THE VINTNER'S VIXEN

THE RIVER HILL SERIES

REBECCA NORINNE

JAMAILA BRINKLEY

Welcome to River Hill, where the only thing more intoxicating than the wine is the man who makes it.

With movie roles for "curvy best friend" drying up fast, actress Angelica Travis is happy to leave Hollywood behind to renovate a bed and breakfast in River Hill, the jewel of Northern California's wine country. She's got plans and power tools ready, but an inconvenient attraction to her handsome new neighbor is **not** on the agenda.

Winemaker Noah Bradstone's master plan is right on schedule until construction on the B&B next door threatens his prize-winning grapes. His only choice is to confront his sexy new neighbor, but with her pink toolbelt and quick retorts, she's the single most infuriating woman he's ever met. What's even more infuriating is that he wants her anyway.

Despite their constant bickering, Angelica and Noah discover they have more in common than they initially thought—including an attraction that burns red hot. But when his past and her future collide, they're forced to answer some very difficult questions about their relationship. Can their love survive a pair of shocking revelations? Better yet, can they survive each other?

"*The Vintner's Vixen* was so much more than I was expecting. I figured it was going to be a formulated RomCom I could curl up with and laugh my way through. In some ways it was...until it wasn't and I enjoyed it even more for that." — Mean Girls Luv Books

CONTENTS

CHAPTER ONE

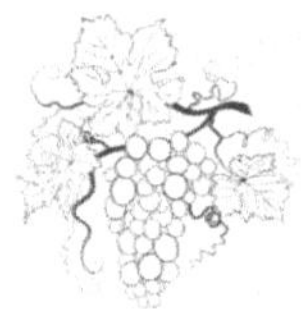

Having grown up with a mother who planned the family's annual summer trip based on her astrologer's divinations (excellent ones, to her credit), Noah Bradstone might have developed a healthy respect for the mystic and unknown.

You could think that, but you'd be wrong.

So when the universe—in its infinite wisdom—tried to tell him it was a bad idea to get out of bed that morning, he'd glibly ignored the signs.

The first was when he was yanked out of a perfectly marvelous dream involving himself, Joan Holloway from *Mad Men*, and a bottle of fine Kentucky bourbon by the caustic smell of diarrhea wafting into his bedroom. It turned out that Molly, his sweet brown Labrador retriever, had somehow eaten the entire box of donuts he'd planned to bring into the tasting room later that morning. It was the second time that month she'd eaten something she shouldn't have, which also meant it was the second time he'd had to get down on his hands and knees to scrub runny shit stains out of his antique Turkish rug.

And the second sign?

While knee deep in dog feces, his phone began to ring off the hook. He tossed his rubber gloves into a bucket of murky brown water and checked to make sure his hands were clean before picking up the device. Seven missed calls—all before seven o'clock in the morning. He swiped his finger across the screen and groaned when he saw who'd been frantically trying to reach him.

Noah loved his mother—truly, he did—but with his thirty-fifth birthday fast approaching and no sign of a wife on the horizon (much less a girlfriend), Bernice Winchester Bradstone, scion of San Francisco society, was becoming *restless*. With Noah's two younger sisters married off to men the family matriarch had practically hand-picked for them, her focus was now firmly placed on achieving the same for her dawdling son. No matter that he'd told her repeatedly he didn't want, or need, her help—in his love life or otherwise. But with the city's famed Founders' Ball weeks away, there was no doubt in Noah's mind that was why she was calling.

Instead of returning her calls, Noah flicked the phone's ringer to silent and made his way to the large walk-in shower in his master bedroom. His day might have started off shitty—*pun absolutely intended*—but he wasn't about to let his dream date with the luscious Miss Holloway go to waste.

An hour later Noah was in his trusty, beat up Ford F-150, making his way down the long, winding dirt drive that separated his property from his neighbor's, when he saw a large plume of dust rising up in the distance. Pushing his sunglasses up, he craned his neck forward to get a better look out the windshield. He tried to make out where the disturbance originated, but it was too far away—he couldn't quite tell if it was coming from his land or old Mrs. Winthrop's. He hadn't scheduled anyone to work in that particular field today and, as far as he knew, the estate was still vacant after his neighbor's death a few months ago.

The closer he drove, the more pronounced the dirt cloud became, until he was less than five hundred feet from where a crew was digging up vines and tossing them in a large discard pile in the middle of the drive.

"Holy fuck!" he exclaimed when he realized what he was seeing. He hit the gas, and tires spun in the dry dirt before finding purchase.

A few short seconds later, Noah slammed his truck to a stop and leaped out of the cab, reaching into the bed to pull out a tire iron. "What the *fuck* do you think you're doing?!" He bore down on the crew with the make-shift weapon fisted in his right hand and rage clouding his vision.

The wine industry was made up of all types of people. Some would give you the shirt off their backs if they thought it would help, while others would smile in your face and then stab you in the back the second you turned away. Still, in all the years his family had been in the business, he'd never heard of someone tearing out someone else's vines.

An older, grizzled man stepped forward and crossed his large, beefy arms over his chest. "And you are?"

"I'm the owner of those vines!" Noah hollered, pointing at the increasingly large pile. "And you have about two seconds to explain what the fuck you're doing on my land before I start bashing some skulls in." He wasn't a violent man. In fact, aside from a couple of schoolyard skirmishes from his days at prep school, he'd never been in a fight in his life. But at that moment, he didn't care that it was essentially one against five, and that each man in front of him had at least forty pounds on him. They'd just destroyed hundreds of thousands of dollars worth of award-winning pinot noir and he didn't have the first clue why.

The foreman raised his eyebrow at Noah as if to ask, 'You and what army?' before turning around and grabbing a clipboard from one of his crew. "You don't look like Angelica Travis."

"Who?" Noah stared at the man. "I don't know anyone by that name. My name's Noah Bradstone and those—" he pointed at the pile "—are my mother-fucking grapes, and you're standing on my goddamn land!"

What the fuck was wrong with these people?

"I don't know what you're talking about," the foreman drawled, flipping through page after page. Eventually, he found the one he was looking for and passed the clipboard to Noah. "But I have a work order from Mrs. Calliope Winthrop's estate to clear this plot of land up to the property line so the new owner—that'd be Miz Travis—can widen the drive."

Noah examined the diagram and then tossed the clipboard to the ground, exasperated. "You've got to be fucking kidding me." He kicked at the damn thing and missed.

"Now wait just a minute!" the foreman snapped, picking up his paperwork and dusting it off with one big, callused hand. Stepping closer, he pointed menacingly at Noah's chest as the rest of the crew took two steps forward. "I don't know what your goddamn problem is, but I will not have you strolling up and yelling at me and my crew. I was paid to do a job and that's what I'm doing."

Looking to the heavens, Noah counted to three in an attempt to bring his anger under control. He dropped his hands and faced the other man. "Those schematics are laid out *upside down*." He pointed to the opposite side of the drive. "*Those* are the grapes you were supposed to pull out." And then he pointed at his land—his precious, marred vineyard. "*That* is my land. And what you just did cost me a couple hundred thousand dollars in lost revenue. Those vines in that produce the best fucking pinot noir in the country."

He blew out a long breath and linked his fingers behind his head. Marching a couple of paces away, he tried to wrap his mind around what he should do next. Finally, he turned back toward the foreman. "Look, I know you were just doing your job, but I'm going to need your business card all the same."

The man visibly bristled as his crew muttered behind him. "You can't sue me!"

"Maybe not," Noah answered. "But I sure as hell can sue Mrs. Winthrop's idiot fucking grandkids and whoever drew up those plans. So ... like I said, I'm going to need your name." Noah notched his chin. "And I'll be taking that clipboard with me."

"You'll be doing no such thing!" the foreman responded indignantly, tossing it to a member of his crew.

Noah sighed. "Fine, have it your way." He pulled his phone from his pocket and took a photo of the truck parked on the side of the drive—the one that had a large advertisement for Jesse's Landscaping and Maintenance emblazoned on the driver's side door. "I don't know if you're Jesse or if that's your boss, but one of you should expect to hear from my lawyers. Now, if you don't mind, I'll ask you to kindly get the fuck off my property." Noah bent down and picked up the tire iron before crossing his arms over his chest and staring the other man down.

"Fine." The foreman nodded. "I've got no skin in this game. C'mon guys." He motioned for his crew to follow and then they climbed into his large truck and pulled away.

Standing in a cloud of kicked up dirt, Noah looked over his prized grapes and sighed. He didn't have the first fucking clue what to do now. They hadn't covered this sort of thing at UC Davis. Sure, winegrowers ripped out vines all the time—ones that weren't producing as well as they should be, or to make room for new grapes when one style fell out of favor—but he'd never heard of a situation like this. You just didn't do that sort of thing. Not when a winemaker had everything riding on a certain crop from a particular vineyard.

Like he did.

Clearly the universe was trying to tell him something. Noah just wished he knew what the fuck it was. The day had started out badly, he'd just never expected it to get *this* bad.

With another weighty sigh, he thumbed the screen on his phone and brought up his contacts. Scrolling, he came to the only name he could think of who could advise him on what to do now. He hated making this call almost as much as he hated the idea of having to talk to his mother later on. If there were two people who knew how to push his buttons, it was his mom and his dad, the famous cult winemaker Carter Bradstone.

Noah didn't have a bad relationship with his father, per se. By most standards, you could even say they were close. But when Noah had decided to strike out on his own, some harsh words had been said—from both sides. He loved his father, and he loved the man's wines too; they just weren't the types of wine *he* wanted to make himself.

And what's more, he hadn't wanted to wait years to take over as the head winemaker at Bradstone Family Vineyards, only to be constantly compared to his legendary father. He knew he could never change the style of wines the vaunted family winery was famous for, so instead of taking his 'rightful' spot by his father's side, when he'd turned twenty-five, Noah had cashed in his trust to buy his own vineyards from a wine-maker who was retiring. His father had been less than impressed with the idea.

Now, ten years later, Noah's gamble had paid off, but his father still had a hard time treating him as an equal. Or, if not equal, then at least a major player in his own right. No matter what Noah did or what he managed to accomplish, it always felt like his dad would see him as an upstart who'd eschewed legacy and tradition to cash in on consumer whims. Noah knew in his heart that hadn't been the case, and the awards and accolades he'd begun receiving the last couple of years validated his instincts, but where family and business was concerned, sometimes cooler heads couldn't prevail.

Still, there was no one more seasoned than Carter Bradstone when it came to dealing with surprises. While his father had never experienced something *quite* like this, he'd seen his fair share of ruined crops in the thirty-plus years he'd been in business. Noah knew he'd have some valuable advice.

At this point, all was lost—there was nothing he could do to salvage the vines—so he needed to think about what came next. With the runaway success of his last bottling of Prodigy Pinot Noir, he'd built expectations around what he was capable of delivering. Now, except for the liquid that was already bottled and laying down, he had nothing left to deliver. He needed a game plan, and much to his chagrin, that meant he needed someone with more experience.

Bracing himself, Noah dialed his father's number and waited for the man to answer. Taking a deep breath, he swallowed his pride and said, "Dad? It's Noah. I need your help."

W
ith his destroyed vines hauled away, Noah shook Vincent Casilla's hand and wished the man well. "Thanks for helping me out," he said, walking the older man to his car. "I appreciate it."

Vincent shook his head glumly. "Such a goddamn shame. Those vines were at least forty years old."

"You're telling me," Noah agreed with a derisive snort. "Looks like my Prodigy Pinot was the last of its kind."

"On the plus side, kid, this might propel remaining inventory into rarified air. Once word gets out that these grapes are gone, there's going to be a run on what's left. You know how the collectors get."

Noah *did* know how the collectors got. So did Vincent, having been his father's vineyard manager for the last twenty years. Next to his father, Noah trusted Vincent's insight more than anyone else's. He'd started out as a day laborer when he'd first come to the United States, but Carter had taken Vincent under his wing and taught the man everything he knew about growing grapes. Now the two acted as a well-oiled machine, producing wine that graced virtually every table on the West Coast.

"Which would be all well and good if any of that money ever saw its way back to me."

"True, but you've seen what happens once your wine gets added to one of those lists. You can't keep up with the demand. And trust me, this is going to get out. By the way, your dad wanted me to offer you his press team to get ahead of the news."

"Nah, that's all right," Noah said. "I'll take care of it."

That was another way he differed from his father. While every little thing Bradstone Family Vineyards did was announced via a press release, Noah relied on social media channels to talk directly to the people who cared most about his wines: the customers.

Sure, a press release was good to put out when Robert Parker scored your wine a ninety-nine—but for everything else, he took to Facebook and Instagram. Lord knew he'd taken enough pictures of the day's carnage for the insurance report (and potential lawsuit he was already considering) to write a whole tome about the demise of his beloved grapevines. Now he just needed to make sure he could post without using every expletive in his vocabulary to describe the negligent new owner of the old house next door and the assholes who were responsible.

"Thanks again," Noah added as his old friend climbed into the cab of his own truck.

"Anytime," Vincent offered, his hand hanging out the window in a friendly wave as he drove down the drive, turning at the road in the direction of the neighboring valley and Bradstone Family Vineyards.

Alone with nothing but his thoughts and righteous anger, Noah huffed out a loud breath and ran his hands through his hair. This was *not* how he'd anticipated spending his morning and afternoon, and the day wasn't quite over yet. Right before Vincent had pulled up, he'd made another phone call, this one to cancel a meeting he was very much looking forward to.

While on principle Noah hated canceling meetings, this particular one rankled even more. Naomi Klein wasn't just the artist who designed his bottle labels, she was also one of his closest friends. And a little more, sometimes. They'd been friends since they were kids forced to endure the ridiculous traditions and affectations that came with being a part of the San Francisco elite.

If Noah had hated all the times he'd had to don a tuxedo, Naomi had gotten the worst of it. As her parents' youngest child and only daughter, all of her mother's hopes and dreams for social success had been pinned on Naomi. Her debutante ball had been larger and more grandiose than any they'd seen before or since. Noah acting as her escort for that horrible affair had cemented their friendship forever. Here they were, almost twenty years later, still enjoying each other's company. These days, though, they didn't keep it quite as innocent as they had back when they'd been sixteen.

Not that he and Naomi were a couple—much to his mother's chagrin. Aside from her "advancing age," Naomi was *exactly* the type of woman his parents would love to see him settle down with. After all, she had the right name, pedigree, education, and family connections. But that wasn't the type of relationship they enjoyed. The two were friends first and foremost; they just happened to enjoy each other's bodies every now and again as well. That they'd been able to maintain such an unconventional friendship all these years astounded the rest of their mutual friends, but it worked for them and he'd been looking forward to mixing a little business with pleasure with her this afternoon.

Unfortunately, now he had *other* business to attend to. Namely, driving up to the dilapidated home next door to see if the new owner, this Angelica Travis person, was around so he could give her a piece of his mind.

"Angelica, that place is a dump."

"It isn't." Angelica Travis turned her phone away from the building and stared into the exasperated brown eyes of her agent, Jai Carter. "It's just … dilapidated. No, weatherworn." That was a good word. Pleased, she smiled fondly at phone and new home alike.

The house nestled comfortingly at the end of a long, swooping gravel drive lined with grapevines. Its front porch was sagging, and the roof drooped a little, but the columns that supported it were strong. A pair of ancient oak trees flanked the sprawling two-story building, which had been added onto during different periods in its long life. The main section was classic Colonial, with faded white shingle siding marching determinedly past green-shuttered windows. To the left, some former owner had gone Swiss: a stuccoed addition featured chalet-style timber framing and a wooden roof with decorative gables. Appropriate for her former home in one of L.A.'s more creative neighborhoods, maybe, but not so much here in wine country. The addition on the right side of the house was older, and whoever had put it up had at least made more of an effort for it to blend in. But Craftsman-style woodwork and harsh Frank Lloyd Wright angles didn't give a wine country vibe any more than the chalet addition did. It was no wonder she'd gotten this place so cheap.

"It has bathrooms for every bedroom," she told Jai. "And the property is surrounded by vineyards. You've got to come out here. It's incredible."

"You know what's incredible? The view from my condo."

"You don't know what you're missing."

"Judging by what I just saw, a hell of a lot of work." His voice softened, and she knew he was trying his best to stay positive—for her sake.

She and Jai had been friends for years, through her entire career really … or what there was of it. He'd signed her as a starving model fresh off the plane from New York and helped her build a name for herself in romantic comedies as she'd gained confidence as an actress. And weight. Which was why all of her roles in the last few years had been relegated to "curvy best friend" status. Some sassy, some serious, although none of them lead material. But he'd gotten her great money for them, and he was the person she trusted most in the world.

"Are you sure about this, Angelica?"

She nodded. "I can do this." She aimed the phone at her waist. "Look, I even have a tool belt."

"It's pink."

"Tool belts can be pink."

"Honey, anything can be pink. That doesn't mean you know how to use it."

"Jai, please try not to be a dick."

"I'm not—"

"Remember my first place?" she asked quickly. When he nodded, she squinted into the phone. "Did I, or did I not, renovate it?"

"Angelica, you had the kitchen redone."

"And I did a damn good job of it." She'd sold that place for nearly twice what she'd paid for it, and the new owners had scored a feature in some architectural magazine later.

"Your contractors did."

"I did some of it."

He sighed. "I'm not saying you didn't. I'm just staying you don't have a lot of experience with—" he waved his hand "—structural stuff."

She looked back at her investment. It did look somewhat … unstructured. She firmed her chin in determination. "I can do this."

"Can I at least send you the name of the guy Greg used to take out that wall in the condo?"

"Jai, what good is a contractor in L.A. going to do me in Sonoma County?"

"I don't know, honey; I don't know anything about contractors."

"You should probably leave the hard work to me, then." She paused, distracted by a distant rumbling. "What is that?"

"What's what? Hey! Stop spinning the phone! You know I get seasick."

"Yes, it's too bad," she said absently. "That yacht in Cannes last year was pretty epic."

"Sure, rub it in."

A beat-up Ford was barreling down her driveway, spraying gravel as it went. More vindication that she'd been right to ask the sellers to clear space to widen the drive so it could be paved, she thought.

She'd gotten a call this morning from their real estate agent saying the company they'd hired was finally getting it done. She loved grapevines, but it wasn't like the ones on her property were producing anything like the ones next door. Clearing a few wasn't going to hurt her aesthetic values.

The truck slid to a stop and she smiled as she saw the cheerful tongue of a brown lab peeking out the passenger side window. Maybe this was a local contractor who'd heard she'd bought the place and wanted to be first in line to try to sell her his services. Well, all right. She probably was going to need some help, at least with the porch and the roof. And maybe covering the stucco.

And then the driver got out, and her mouth went utterly dry. The single most beautiful man she'd ever met, including four years modeling and ten spent in Hollywood, was striding toward her.

And he was *pissed.*

"Who the hell are you?" His gaze traveled from her face down to her waist, where it stopped on her pink tool belt. His heavy brows drew even further down. "Oh, you have got to be kidding me."

Well, that was enough to break the spell. Angelica scowled. "Excuse me?"

"Please tell me you're not the new owner," he said.

She shoved her phone in her pocket and put her hands on her hips. "And if I am?"

"If you are, you and I have a problem." The dog scratched at the window of the truck, and the man made a sharp motion with his hand. "Not now, Molly."

"A problem?" Angelica glanced at the dog. She could hear pitiful whining. "You should let her out."

"You should mind your own damn business," he snapped. "And get a handle on your fucking contractors."

She hoped the dog peed on his seats. "I don't have any contractors." She stepped forward, ignoring the fact that he had a good foot on her. "You want to tell me what you're doing on my property, mister?" She'd had enough of dickheads talking down to her during her years in Hollywood. No way in hell was some asshole with a cute dog going to come to her house and start making demands.

He pressed his fingers to the bridge of his nose. It was a nice nose, she noted. Sort of elegant and patrician. Too bad it was on a psychopath's face. "You *do* have contractors," he said. "Some landscaping company. I took a picture." He pulled his phone out of his pocket and swiped a few times. "Here. Jesse, or somebody he knows." He held out the phone.

She peered at a picture of a van she'd never seen before. "I don't know who that is."

"Well, they think you do," he snapped. "And they just pulled out more than a quarter million dollars' worth of vines about half a mile that way." He pointed back down the driveway.

Angelica frowned. "Wait, this is about pulling out the vines?" His exaggerated sigh annoyed her further. "Those vines are on my property, you moron."

"No, they aren't. They're on mine. And don't call me a moron." He loomed over her and she found herself staring at a nicely muscled chest that wasn't much hidden by his t-shirt.

Unimpressed, she poked him. "Step away."

"Ow!"

She smirked. She'd had her nails done yesterday. They matched the tool belt, of course. "I don't know who you are, but you've got it wrong."

"I'm Noah Bradstone. Your neighbor. And no, I don't." He flipped through his phone again and aimed the screen accusingly at her. "See?"

"They tore out the vines so that the driveway could be widened and paved," she explained patiently. "The sellers arranged it as part of the contract. I'm turning this place into a B&B."

"Yes, I know."

"So there's no problem." She smiled up at him, the kind of smile that usually made men remember it came from somebody with killer curves.

He seemed unmoved. "There *is* a problem. They tore out the wrong vines."

She blinked. "What?"

His face might have been carved of stone for all it moved. Really handsome stone. "They. Tore. Out. The. Wrong. Vines."

Shit. "Where? Can you show me?" The glow was starting to come off of her sparkling first day here.

He nodded. "Pictures, or in person?" He held up the phone.

"How far?"

"The end of your drive," he said. "Where it splits off from my back road."

She sighed. "Let me get my car."

"Just hop in." He gestured toward the truck.

She raised her eyebrows at him, and he actually reddened a little. "I'll let her out." He crossed over to the passenger door and opened it. The brown dog leapt down and wiggled her way around him in a happy circle. Angelica hid a smirk as he surreptitiously patted the seat down before ordering the dog to go pee in the bushes.

The dog—Molly—ignored him and came straight for Angelica, who knelt to greet her. "Well, hello, beautiful," she said, scratching a pair of floppy ears and dodging an enthusiastic tongue. "You can come hang out with me anytime you like."

Molly's owner snorted. "Yeah, right."

Angelica straightened and scowled at him again. "Let's get this over with."

He nodded, then gestured Molly into the back of the truck with a whistle. The dog gave Angelica's hand one last lick and trotted over to him. Angelica followed and was surprised when he opened the passenger door for her after giving Molly's scrabbling back legs a quick boost.

"Thanks," Angelica said automatically as she seated herself.

"You're welcome," he murmured absently as he frowned at her house. "Here you go." He shut the door as she clicked her seatbelt on, and she frowned too. Rough and ready farm types didn't usually open doors for women, did they? Not that she was complaining.

The truck rumbled to life underneath her, and she stole a few glances at him as they sat in awkward silence for the five minutes it took to drive to the end of her lane. He had dark hair and dark eyes in a tanned face, some of which was hidden by facial hair that she couldn't quite determine the intent of. Was it a short beard? Or was he just scruffy? Either way, she could feel herself warming as she looked him over. Not good. *No time for that*, she told herself sternly. *Especially not with somebody who might sue you.*

"Here," he said, pulling to a stop.

She looked out the window. It looked … like land-scapers had been there. She frowned. "Wait—"

"Have you figured it out?" His voice was snide.

She shot him a withering look as she got out of the truck, leaving the door open in case Molly wanted to jump back in. Her feet crunched on the gravel and she put a hand onto the side of the vehicle for balance. No need for a twisted ankle today, thank you.

A sudden wetness made her look up to see Molly's cheerful face, tongue bathing her hand. "Gee, thanks, Molly." She pulled away and went to investigate the carnage. Specifically, the carnage on the left side of the drive. Not the right. Which was what she'd asked for, since the property line ran pretty closely alongside the driveway on the left.

Somehow, somebody had screwed up. And judging by Noah Bradstone's expression, the buck stopped with her.

"They were supposed to clear that side." She pointed.

"Yes, I know. The foreman had a diagram that was clearly wrong," Noah said.

"How much—" she gulped. "How much damage is it?"

He pressed his hand to his forehead again. "It's a lot."

She closed her eyes. "Can you give me some time to come up with a solution?"

"What the hell kind of solution can you possibly

come up with? These vines are irreplaceable!" His voice was rising again.

"Well, I wasn't offering to replace them," she snapped. "There's been a mistake, but I had nothing to do with making it. I'm trying to help you, here."

"Some help."

"Forget it." She stormed back to the truck and slammed the passenger door shut. No way was she riding back with him. "I'll call the sellers' agent to find out how this happened, and then I'll call the contractors to figure out who's liable. In the meantime, you can get the hell off of my property."

"With pleasure," he said. "And you can stay off of mine. Rest assured, you'll be hearing from my lawyer." He got back into the truck and fired up the engine.

"You and your lawyer can bite me!" Her shout didn't have much impact on the dust cloud his tires kicked up as he drove away. She looked back up the driveway. It was half a mile back to the house, at least. "Fuck."

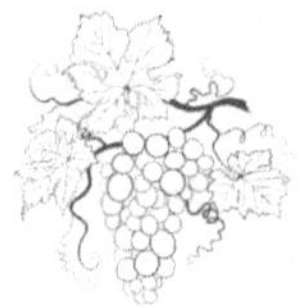

CHAPTER THREE

"What crawled up your ass and died?" Chef Max Vergaras asked, sliding Noah a cocktail when he pulled a stool up to his favorite spot at his favorite restaurant, Frankie's on the River. Frankie's was Max's pride and joy, the culmination of his entire career, and Noah had been coming here ever since his friend had taken over the space.

Noah slammed the whole drink back, his throat working overtime, without stopping to savor the smoky undertones of whiskey laced with plump, fresh blackberries from Max's garden out back. "You would not believe the day I've had," he replied, swiping the back of his hand across his mouth. "You know I love your cocktails, but I'm going to need the hard stuff tonight to wind down from the epic shit storm I'm drowning in right now."

"That sounds ominous," Max observed.

"You know the old Winthrop estate?"

"Yeah," Max answered, wiping down the already gleaming copper bar. "What about it?"

"It finally sold."

"No shit?"

"Yup. Which I couldn't care about one way or the other, except the new owner decided to widen the driveway between our properties and the contractors she hired to remove those stupid fucking Concord grapes screwed up and pulled out three rows of my pinot noir ones instead." Noah shook his head solemnly. He could have lived without the Viognier, but the loss of his prized pinot noir was a goddamned travesty.

Max dropped his rag and stared at Noah like he'd sprouted two heads. "You're fucking kidding."

"I wish I was, man. I really fucking wish I was."

"How does something like that even happen?"

"Best I can tell, old lady Winthrop's grandkids fucked up when they drew up the plans, and when the new owner signed off on the work, she didn't bother checking to make sure everything was correct." Noah rubbed the spot between his eyebrows in an effort to forestall the migraine that had been threatening to form all afternoon.

"Idiot," Max bit out in anger. "Let me guess. She's some bored, rich housewife who thinks the world revolves around her? She probably wanted you to thank her for the work. Or worse, pay her for it."

Noah could forgive Max the assumption. Last year, he'd been involved with a woman going through a long, bitter divorce. They'd even talked about getting married once it eventually came through, but the moment the ink was dry on the paperwork, she'd dicked him over by running off with her ex-husband's richer best friend, leaving Max with an expensive diamond ring and a broken heart.

"Nah, she's not like that," Noah answered, knowing in his gut he spoke the truth. He didn't know Angelica Travis, but he knew *women*, and he was sure she didn't fall into that camp.

When Max raised a skeptical eyebrow, Noah continued, "Don't get me wrong. She's trouble with a capital T, but it's more the natural disaster, force of nature kind than the scheming, lying bitch kind."

"If you say so," Max responded doubtfully as he shook up another cocktail. Even though Max owned Frankie's—named for the its notorious first owner, a bootlegger named Frankie McShane who'd started a speakeasy on the site during Prohibition—one night a week he left the kitchen in the capable hands of his sous chef so he could hang out behind the bar and chat with customers. "You know my stance on the fairer sex."

"Yeah, and no one here blames you for it." Resting his chin against his fist, Noah added, "I don't actually know what her story is, but I *can* tell you she's in way over her head out there. She's remodeling the place with an aim to turning it into a bed and breakfast." He snorted and leaned back, dropping his hands to rest flat on the copper surface. "She was wearing a pink fucking tool belt, for Christ's sake!"

"Oh, that must have been cute." Max laughed.

The thing was—and Noah hated to admit it—it *had* been cute. More than cute, in fact. Angelica Travis might be a menace to society, but she was the most mouthwatering menace he'd ever seen. Her blonde hair, porcelain skin, and high cheekbones were the first things he'd noticed about her, but then his eyes had traveled downward to take in each rise and fall of her bountiful curves. In a plain white v-neck t-shirt and ratty, paint-splattered jeans slung low on her luscious hips, he'd had to do a double take.

Simply put, Miss Angelica Travis—God, he hoped it was *Miss* Travis—was his wildest fantasy made flesh. And what lovely flesh it was.

"It was something, all right," he answered with a shake of his head. "I won't lie. She's beautiful, and I wouldn't mind getting my hands on her for a night, but she's quite possibly the most aggravating person I've ever met as well."

He looked up from his drink to find Max's eyes trained on something—or someone—across the room. Noah swiveled on his stool to see what had captured his friend's attention and let out a frustrated groan. "You've got to be kidding me," he muttered, tossing the rest of the whiskey down his throat. Wincing at the burn as it traveled down his esophagus, he said, "Not here, too."

Max laughed and poured Noah another shot. "I take it that's the new neighbor?"

"In the flesh."

"And what lovely flesh it is," Max muttered appreciatively.

"You took the words right out of my mouth." With a grimace, Noah asked, "Why does someone so goddamned beautiful have to be so much trouble?"

"Good luck with that. By the looks of things, you're going to need it." Max strolled away, his eyes fixed on Angelica as he went.

Noah craned his neck to cast a covert glance her way and tried not to stare—too hard. She'd changed out of her work clothes and into a halter top that hugged her curves that she'd paired with a pleated skirt that skimmed just above her knees, giving Noah a small peek of her shapely thighs. She'd taken down her ponytail, too, and her long, blonde hair cascaded down her back in thick, bouncy waves. If she was going for the whole Marilyn Monroe look, Noah thought, she'd nailed it perfectly.

With one final perusal of her ample assets, Noah swiveled back around and resumed imbibing his drink. He could admire Angelica's beauty, but that didn't mean he wanted her to catch him in the act. Besides, it was bad enough he would have to interact with her in a professional capacity; he didn't want her invading his personal life, too.

Noah loved living in a small town, but this was one of those times he missed the anonymity of San Francisco. Not that he had any intention of ever moving back there, much to his mother's chagrin. So it was just as well then when Angelica settled herself at a small table on the other side of the restaurant, far away from him.

A stool scraped along the reclaimed hardwood floors and Sean Amory, River Hill's resident baker, joined Noah at the bar. Sean's family owned The Breadery, the bakery that was located across from Frankie's on River Hill's picturesque town square. Noah had been friends with Sean for years, but he'd only recently moved home to work at the family business. He and Noah made a point of meeting up for drinks at least one night a week, usually when Sean didn't have to be up before dawn to fire up the bakery's ovens, and preferably on one of Max's behind-the-bar nights.

"Heard about your drama earlier," Sean remarked, popping a small handful of nuts into his mouth.

Of course he had, Noah thought. "Fucking small town gossips," he muttered as he took another sip of his whiskey.

"You could always move back to San Francisco," Sean answered, hailing a bartender to order a beer.

"You and Max must have been clairvoyants in another life. You're both mind readers tonight."

"You don't exactly have a poker face, man."

Noah chuckled. "No, I don't suppose I do."

Sean propped his forearms on the copper bar top.

"You're not seriously considering moving back, are you?"

Noah waved away his friend's concern. "You know I hated living there. I was only thinking how much easier it is to enjoy a drink in peace when you don't have to worry about running into someone you don't want to. It's easier to hide out in the city."

Sean raised the bottle to his lips and threw back a swig. "And I take it you're hoping to hide from the infamous new neighbor?"

Noah's eyes darted to the corner of the restaurant where Angelica was busy reviewing the menu. "Among others," he confirmed.

"You know who she is, don't you?"

"You mean besides the world's biggest menace?"

Sean laughed, his dimples forming deep hollows in his smooth face. He might have left L.A. behind weeks ago, but with gleaming white teeth and a hard, chiseled jaw, he'd forever look the part of smooth Hollywood playboy. He'd been a record executive, but he'd often been mistaken for a movie or TV star instead. "You really don't know, do you?"

Noah shrugged. "Haven't a clue."

"Dude. When was the last time you went to the movies, or turned on the TV?"

Noah twisted in his stool to face his friend. "You know I don't have a television."

Sean's eyebrow lifted while he waited for Noah to answer his other question.

Scrubbing a hand over his face, Noah said, "What

year did the last Indiana Jones movie come out? The one with the aliens?"

Sean rolled his eyes and shook his head. "It was a crystal skull, not an alien. And because you didn't know that was *last decade*, I'm guessing you also didn't see the remake of *Clueless* a few years back."

Noah's head shot back in disbelief. "Why the fuck would they remake *Clueless*? The original was just fine. I mean, it's no Hitchcock or Scorsese, but really? *Clueless?*"

Sean chuckled. "Yeah, and you're probably not going to believe this, but your new neighbor played Tai in the remake."

"No way," Noah responded, trying to match the curvy blonde beauty he'd met earlier that afternoon with the awkward, homely character he remembered from the original. "I don't believe you."

"Here, see for yourself." Sean pulled out his phone and brought up his IMDB app. Locating the remake's listing, he passed the device to Noah and then hailed a waitress to put in two orders of the restaurant's famous pork belly tacos with mango and papaya salsa.

"Well, I'll be damned," Noah mused, passing the phone back to his friend. "That's not what she looks like now, I'll tell you that much for nothing."

He had a hard time reconciling the human wrecking ball he'd met that morning with the gawky woman whose picture he'd just seen. He supposed if you squinted really hard you could make out the resemblance, but *that* Angelica was missing the luscious curves Noah had admired so much, and her shiny blonde hair had been dyed a dull, dishwater brown. He didn't even want to consider how they'd made it look like she'd permanently stuck her finger in a light socket.

"You don't need to tell me," Sean answered. "Woman's a chameleon. If memory serves, she made a career out of playing the dorky best friend or an awkward sidekick." His brows furrowed in concentration as he took a bite of his taco. Chewing around his food, he added, "Haven't seen much of her lately though, come to think of it."

Noah's head turned, and his eyes landed on Angelica who—much to his horror—was staring right back at him. With a gleam in her eye he could see all the way across the room, she lifted her glass of wine in salute. Noah nodded gruffly, and turned back around. Eating his taco in large bites, he'd nearly consumed the whole thing when Max re-joined them.

"What are you two ladies gossiping about?" he asked, leaning his forearms on the copper surface.

"I was bringing Noah up to speed on who his pretty new neighbor is."

"Stunner, ain't she?" Max asked with a raise of his brow.

Sean nodded and finished off his beer. "And exactly his type, too."

"Fuck you," Noah interjected. "I don't have a type."

"Hate to break it to you, man, but yes, you do."

Noah crossed his arms over his chest in defiance. "I'm an equal opportunity lover."

"If you say so," Sean quipped, finishing off his food and pushing his plate away.

Noah glanced between his two smirking friends. Unable to withstand their unrestrained merriment, he finally bit. "Okay, fine. What's my type?"

"Jessica Rabbit," Max answered immediately.

"Christina Hendricks," Sean added, not to be outdone.

"Ashley Graham."

"Sofia Loren."

"Rita Hayworth."

"Kate Upton."

The two men volleyed names of curvy actresses back and forth like a tennis ball until, in unison, they each shouted "Marilyn Monroe!"

Noah had no choice but to laugh at their good-natured ribbing. With a shrug, he said, "Okay, so I like 'em real thick and juicy."

"Ah fuck, he's not quoting Sir Mix-a-Lot again, is he?" Max pushed off the bar and pulled down a bottle of tequila he reserved for nights when the three of them hung out at the restaurant together.

"What?" Noah asked with a grin. "The man knew what he was talking about when it came to tits and ass."

Sean shook his head in mock dismay. "You are the literal worst."

Max passed them each a glass, and they tossed the

smoky liquid back. "Speaking of tits and ass," Max whispered, "she's coming this way."

It was all Noah could do to get the tequila down his throat without choking to death. As it was, he coughed so loud and hard that several patrons turned their heads to make sure he was okay. As Sean pounded him on the back, Noah heard the faint *click-clack* of heels approaching.

"Hello boys," a voice smooth as velvet said from behind him.

Pulling in a gulp of air, he tried his best to inconspicuously wipe the wetness from his eyes. Eventually, he turned to face her, catching a brief glimpse of Max's smirk as he did.

"Hi, Angelica." Noah glanced at his waiting friends, then grudgingly introduced the other two men. "This is Max—this place is his—and that's Sean. He owns the bakery down the street. Guys, this is my new neighbor, Angelica Travis. She's the one who bought old Mrs. Winthrop's estate." Noah hoped Max and Sean would play along and not give away the fact that they'd already known who she was well before his introduction.

Angelica nodded at each man in turn. "Max. Sean." Then her gaze flickered between the three of them as the right side of her cherry lips hitched up in a coy smile. "A rugged chef, a handsome baker, and ... a grumpy winemaker."

Noah didn't know why, but he'd been holding his breath as she described what she saw when she looked at them, wondering what adjective she'd bestow upon him. When instead of lauding his appearance as she had his friends, she picked apart his personality, he had to fight to control his disappointment. He was man enough to admit that both Max and Sean were good looking guys, but he was too, goddamnit.

For several more minutes, she traded small talk with Sean and Max while Noah sat in mostly brooding silence. Lest she think she'd hurt his feelings, he made sure to inject himself into the conversation here and there, but he didn't bother hiding his sigh of relief when she finally turned and strolled away, her mouth-watering hips swinging in temptation.

Noah didn't like Angelica, but he definitely appreciated her appearance.

"You want another one?" Max asked, drawing Noah's attention back to the conversation.

"Nah, I'm good." Between the cocktail he'd slammed back when he'd first arrived, and then the whiskey and tequila, he'd already pushed the limits of what was acceptable on a work night. "I think I'll have another taco and then I'll head out."

"Good idea." Max pushed off the counter and strolled to the window of the kitchen to place the order directly.

Sean reached across the bar to grab a fistful of peanuts. "I think your Sir Mix-a-Lot might be on to something."

"Oh yeah, what's that?" Noah wasn't following the sudden shift in conversation.

Sean tilted his head to indicate the direction Angelica had departed and cackled. "Because that woman most definitely has an L.A. face with an Oakland booty."

Noah groaned at his play on the famous rap song, but he wasn't about to argue. Because the truth was Angelica Travis was little in the middle but she had much back.

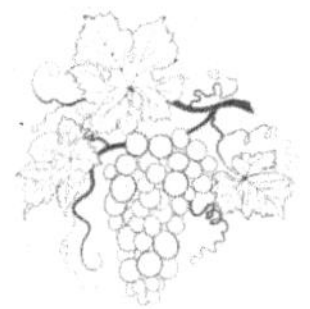

CHAPTER FOUR

*S*he'd lost her nerve, damn it. Angelica scowled down at her wine glass. She'd had every intention of approaching Noah with a reasonable business proposition, but damn if he hadn't unsettled her with that brooding stare and all those gorgeous muscles peeking through the collar of his shirt.

Not to mention the company he was keeping. How on earth could one small town contain so many gorgeous men? And how was it fair that they were all such good friends? It was a wonder the women of River Hill didn't just line up outside the door of this restaurant every night.

Although … she glanced around, noting the full tables and bustling servers. Maybe they did. Who could blame them?

She stole another glance at the three men as she took a sip of the truly excellent wine. It was like watching a wall of walking sex. Noah still stood out, though. Probably because his friends were laughing, and he was still … grumpy. She felt her lips quirk into a smile. She hadn't missed his reaction to her little jab. The thought of his annoyance sobered her, though.

It was her fault he'd had such a bad day, after all. Kind of. Technically, it was Mrs. Winthrop's obnoxious grandchildren's fault, but after the pittance she'd paid them for her beloved new property, she wasn't about to try to drag them back here.

So she had to talk to Noah. And this time, she'd stay on task.

No muscles. Ignore the five-o-clock shadow, Angelica. Stop imagining his chin scraping your collarbone. Don't look at his hands or think about what his fingers—Damn. She was getting distracted again.

His friends were still ribbing him about something, and he was chuckling reluctantly. Clearly, she wasn't going to get anywhere sieging that fort of manhood. She debated potential strategies for thinning the herd for a moment, then smirked and summoned a waitress. The girl nodded at her request, then headed to Max, the chef, and whispered to him. He turned his dark head toward Angelica, one heavy eyebrow raised, then gave her a brief nod and leaned to the kitchen window.

A few moments later, Angelica watched Noah's gaze follow his tacos as they came out of the kitchen—and straight to her table. The waitress gave her a wink as she deposited the plate and sashayed away, barely avoiding Noah as he stormed over.

"Those are mine," he said. "You make a habit of taking things that aren't yours?"

"Only when they're delicious." She reached out and snagged a piece of pork belly. "Sit and eat."

He scowled. "No thanks." Noah reached for the plate, and she put a hand on it.

"I want to talk to you about something."

He huffed an explosive sigh, but folded his body into the booth opposite her. He tugged the plate out of her grip. "You have until I've inhaled these tacos." He picked the first one up and took a huge bite.

"I want to run something by you. It's about vines."

He swallowed. "Great. Now you're going to set yourself up as competition?"

"Try not to be an idiot," she snapped. "I don't know anything about grapes or growing them."

"Then—"

"For God's sake, Noah, eat your taco and let me finish."

He didn't like not getting the last word, she could tell. Too bad. She'd had enough of men making assumptions about her life and explaining her own ideas to her in Hollywood. There, she'd had to put up with it for the sake of her career. One that had gone down in flames the second she'd gotten to a healthy weight, of course. Cue a lot more explaining from directors, casting agents, and producers, plus a lot of "helpful" suggestions, many of which involved her getting naked. Just not on film.

She shrugged away the memories and focused on

her plan. "Look. I'm sorry about what happened today, and I definitely don't have the kind of money I suspect those vines are worth. But if you're planning on replanting, I have a proposition for you."

His eyebrows shot up, and she felt herself actually blushing for the first time in years. There was an awkward pause, and she realized that he was obeying her command to eat instead of talk. Intriguing.

"I'm still planning on clearing the vines on the other side of the drive to expand it, but only a few feet. There's still an entire field of vines beyond that, and it curves back around behind the house and grounds, too."

She really hadn't intended on buying a small vineyard, but it had come with the house. The tourists would probably love it. She'd originally planned on eventually hiring a gardener to take care of them, but … "Do you know anything about what kind of grapes are planted there?"

He licked a smear of grease off of the base of his thumb, and she swallowed. "Crappy ones," he said dismissively.

"Can you be more specific?"

He shrugged. "Shitty, generic ones is all I'll say. The Winthrops had terrible taste. If you're planning on setting yourself up with a boutique label, you're not going to sell much."

She rolled her eyes. "Seriously? Do I look like I have time to make wine?"

He looked her up and down, and she felt her entire body get hot. "I don't know," he said. "Do you?"

"No. I have a target opening date for the B&B, and I have a lot of renovating to do to get there."

"Good luck with that." He popped the last bite of taco into his mouth and put his hands on the table, getting ready to push himself up to leave.

"Wait! Just hear me out."

He sighed. "What do you want?"

"I want you to grow grapes on my land."

He froze. "What?"

Now that she finally had his real, focused attention, the words came tumbling out. "It doesn't make up for what happened today, but you're going to be replanting anyway, right? I have extra land that I'm not using that's apparently the right kind for growing vines, you have the expertise to do that." He opened his mouth, and she held up a hand. "You'd get the grapes. I don't want them."

His eyes narrowed. "You're offering me free land?"

"I didn't say free."

"You've got to be kidding me. You just cost me a fortune."

"Technically, the Winthrops did. It'd be pretty sticky to come after me, legally." She shrugged, feigning as much indifference as she could in the face of the prospect of a lawsuit and legal fees she definitely couldn't afford, even if she won. "You might win. I might. It's probably not worth it to either of us to fight it out, especially if we can work something out."

"Work something out?"

God, even the language of Hollywood stuck with her. She sounded like the producer who'd offered her a role as an extra in the new *X-Men* movie if she'd let him touch her feet. "It's a business deal, but I'm not trying to make money off you, honestly. I'm thinking a minimal leasing fee and maybe some wine for the B&B once in awhile."

His long fingers drummed on the table as he thought. "The old vines would have to be cleared away."

She'd thought of that already. "If you'll take care of planting new ones, I'll pay to have the old ones cleared."

"That back hill of yours does have some unusually good sunlight hours," he mused. She nodded, trying to look like she knew whether that was relevant or not. He didn't seem fooled. "You want this in writing?"

"Please. Gentlemen's agreements don't really seem to fly these days." Her tone was a little drier than she meant it to be, but his lips quirked into a small smile anyway. Was that a sense of humor peeking through? God, she hoped not. He didn't need anything to make him more attractive—and she didn't sleep with anybody she signed a contract with.

he next morning, Angelica sat in her kitchen, resting her laptop on the butcher block countertop of the temporary island she'd brought from her previous home in L.A. It was the most level thing in the room. She didn't relish trying to balance her coffee mug on the uneven countertops left-over from the seventies. She flipped her browser to the tab she'd left open and admired the pristine Carrera marble for sale at a wholesaler in South San Francisco. She was definitely getting ahead of herself.

Her phone chirped, indicating a video call was coming in. She picked it up and smiled. "Hi, Dad," she said when the screen cleared to reveal her father's worn face.

"I'm here, too!" Her mother's face popped into view, sideways, as she'd shoved her head under her husband's shoulder to fit into the tiny camera screen.

"Hi, Mom. What's up?"

"We wanted to see how you're settling in," her father said.

"How's the weather?" her mother asked.

"The weather is perfect, as always," Angelica answered. "And I'm settling in fine. No issues." She crossed her fingers mentally, remembering the contract that the idea of new countertops had momen-tarily distracted her from reviewing. "How are you two?"

"Never mind us, honey, things are always the same

here," her mother said. "Although I do have a new painting to show you. It might look nice in your B&B!"

Her mother was an incredibly talented artist who'd remained intentionally obscure by making her paintings available only to people she knew and respected. While it wasn't the most effective distribution strategy in terms of profits, it meant her work was valued and appreciated. Jai's office was lined with her paintings, and he frequently received exorbitant offers to buy them from bigwigs and celebrities alike. As far as Angelica knew, he hadn't sold any of them. Neither had Mom, although she could easily have made a living from her work. Instead, she was happy teaching kindergarten.

"I've got a place in the foyer waiting for a painting of yours, Mom," Angelica replied. "And if you come visit when the place is finished, you can decorate the whole thing."

"We have to wait to visit until it's finished?" her father asked. "I have some ideas for your booking software. I was hoping I could come help you test them out." Life at the accounting firm apparently didn't take any time away from his hobby of researching everything in the entire world.

"And I'm pretty good with spackle," her mother added. "Just say the word!"

Angelica rolled her eyes. "I just got the keys yesterday, you two. Cool your jets!"

"As if you don't already have a plan," her mother scoffed.

"I do, but I haven't even cleaned the place yet. You're not coming and staying in a guest room until I've at least had a chance to brighten them up a bit."

"How far is your new place from L.A., again?" Her parents rarely left their comfortable Massachusetts town, and her mother's grasp of California's geography was still slim after more than ten years of her daughter living there.

"Pretty far, Mom." The phone beeped again. Another incoming call. She was popular today, it seemed. "That's Jai. Can I call you back later? I'll take you on a video tour, I promise."

"Say hi to Jai for us!" Her mother loved Jai, and the feeling was mutual. Angelica occasionally wondered if her parents visited to see her, or her agent and his charming husband.

"I will. Bye!" She tapped the 'accept call' button. "Hi, Jai. Calling to tell me how awful my house is?"

"Hello, beautiful." He definitely wanted something. "Actually, I'm calling to take advantage of the awfulness of your house, specifically."

"Beg your pardon?"

"I just had a *very* interesting conversation with somebody named Justin from the Renovation Network."

"I didn't know you watched the Reno Network."

"Greg does."

"Of course he does."

"The point, my sarcastic sweetie, is that I mentioned

your project, and just happened to have some of your headshots handy."

"Recent ones?" She was sick of being told she didn't look like the girl from *Clueless*.

"The newest ones, in all your lush glory."

"Lush? Really?"

"They want to talk to you about following your renovation, Angelica. Series potential."

She caught her breath at those golden words. "Series?" She was done with Hollywood, though. Wasn't she? "I don't know, Jai."

"It's not a movie, Ang." He knew her as well as she knew herself. "It's just you, being you. And think of the publicity for your cute little hotel thing."

"Don't pretend you don't know what a B&B is. Greg asked me for recommendations just last month. I know where you went for your anniversary."

"Don't change the subject."

"It was nice, wasn't it?"

"Of course it was, you have impeccable taste, blah blah blah. Are you interested?"

She fell silent, and Jai did too. She'd wanted her move to River Hill to be a new start, a whole new phase of her life. But was it so wrong to use the experience she'd built up of over a decade of on-camera work give her an edge now? Jai was right about the publicity.

And maybe it was time for a little more honest self-awareness. When she hadn't been disgusted by the behavior in Hollywood, she'd enjoyed the work. She hadn't made a solid career out of nothing, after all.

Maybe she really could combine what she had done before with what she wanted to do now.

Imagining her mother's reaction to seeing her daughter on Reno TV, she smiled. "Let's do it." She flipped her laptop's screen back to the contract Noah's lawyers had drawn up and added her digital signature with a decisive click. "I'm in a contracting mood today. Send it over."

Clicking over to her inbox, Angelica waited for Jai's incoming documents. Out of nowhere, she wondered what Noah would think of having camera crews next door. She'd bet her future Carrera marble counters that he would be … grumpy.

Thump, thump, thump. Boom, boom, boom. Noah stared at the ceiling of his bedroom, the full moon illuminating a slanted path across the wall, as the sound of an unidentifiable pop song's pulsing bass line echoed through the crisp night air. For twenty minutes he lay still, willing the music to quiet, until he couldn't stand another second of it.

Noah knew he had what many would consider questionable taste in music—preferring songs from his college days over anything current—but this was ridiculous. As he sat upright in his bed and ran a frustrated hand through his hair, he heard the faint whisperings of a female voice singing longingly about temptation.

"Goddamnit," he groaned, throwing the covers aside and swinging his legs over the edge of the mattress. He glanced at the clock on his bedside table, glowing green in the dark, and groaned again. It wasn't even eleven o'clock at night but he was about to be *that* guy: the one who was old before his time. The one who warned his new, gorgeous, and exasperating neighbor about people needing to wake up early in the morning ... even on the weekend.

She'd been living next door for six weeks, and he'd seen her around town several times, but this was the first time she'd intruded on his sleep. Well, other than in his dreams, anyway. She was frequently naked in those. But that was besides the point.

Angelica might not understand it, but a farmer's life —because farming he was essentially what he did—was about early mornings and even earlier nights.

Even as he pulled his well-worn jeans up over his naked skin and then buttoned his threadbare flannel over his chest before shoving his feet into a pair of flip-flops, he knew he was about to embark on a fool's errand. Alas, he'd already set himself upon the course, and if anything, he was a man who saw things through.

As he exited the house, Molly raised her head and peered at him, one eye open. "Hey there, girl," Noah whispered. "It's just me."

Hearing her master's voice, she dropped her head back down onto her paws and closed her eyes. For as pampered as she was, once the temperatures got above seventy, Molly preferred to sleep outside under the stars instead of inside with her master. He couldn't begrudge her—if Noah could get away with sleeping outside every night from April to October, he might too. Then again, he really loved his thousand thread count sheets. He might have eschewed his privileged, San Francisco upbringing, but he'd been unable to let go of a few of life's most basic luxuries: a downy feather mattress topper and Frette bed linens among them. Good wine and whiskey were two others.

Hopping into his beat up pickup truck—see, he didn't need *everything* to be fancy—Noah inched down the long, winding drive that separated his property from the Winthrop estate. Scratch that. *Angelica's* place. He still didn't know if she had what it took to remodel that old ramshackle house into something people would pay good money to spend a weekend in, so he cautioned himself not to get too used to thinking of it as hers. Didn't allow himself to think too hard about the possibilities of the hillside vineyard he'd already planned in his head over the last few weeks.

Zinfandel wasn't what Noah was known for—after all, people flocked to Stonewell Vineyards for his Pinot Noir and Bordeaux blends—but that rocky soil with several hours of hot, direct sunshine a day were just itching for the types of vines that could withstand such harsh elements. Noah knew in both his gut and his heart that with the contract Angelica had signed giving him access to her land, he could do something extraordinary. It might not make up for the loss of his vines in the near term, but in the long term, it could prove a watershed moment in his career.

His father had never bothered with Zinfandel; a shame really, since the climate in this revered valley was perfect for it. Hell, the old Italian families who'd come to River Hill in the 1880s from Piemonte, Tuscany, and Campania had recognized those grapes—cousin to their homeland's beloved Sangiovese—would flourish on the slopes leading down to the river. And now, if everything went according to plan, it was Noah's turn to put his stamp on the varietal.

Alas, he didn't want to get too ahead of himself. He still didn't know much about Angelica, but he knew *people*, and if she stuck it out here for even a year, he'd eat his flannel. That pink tool belt she'd worn during their first meeting had told him all he needed to know about his new neighbor, and nothing he'd learned of her in the weeks since had changed his mind about her skillset. Or lack thereof. And when you considered what Sean had told him about her former career in Hollywood, Noah would bet good money this venture was a hobby for her and nothing more.

As Noah's Ford inched its way down the long drive, going slow so as not to kick up too much dirt, he cast his eyes over the hillside in question and tried not to let his imagination run wild. It wasn't too hard, however, to put the brakes on his plans when his headlights flashed over the source of the noise that had kept him up well past his bedtime.

Angelica was sitting in front of a blazing fire on the weathered patio in front of the west wing of her house, surrounded by five—no, make that six—men.

Hopping out of the cab of his truck, he stalked across the yard to stand in front of her, his hands locked on his hips. "Seriously?" he asked, his voice laced with annoyance.

Noah liked to consider himself a self-possessed sort of person, and so he knew exactly why he was irritated. Sure, initially it'd been the music, but now? The spike of displeasure he felt was entirely down to Angelica's cohorts. If it had been, say … he and Max and Sean sitting around the fire with her, he wouldn't have given it a second thought. But he didn't know these men— didn't like the look of them, either—so he was irritated to find her surrounded by a pack of red-blooded American males. And if the empty beer bottles were anything to go by, they were *drunk* males to boot.

"Hello, Noah," Angelica responded dryly, her eyebrow raised as she tipped a bottle back, her throat constricting with each swallow. "Can I help you with something?"

"Do you know what time it is?"

She chuckled. "Actually, I do. Not even midnight yet on a Friday night, if the clock in my kitchen is to be believed." She set the empty bottle down next to her feet as one of the guys popped the cap on a new one and passed it her way.

"Right," Noah clipped, scrubbing a rough hand over his lightly bristled jaw. "The thing is, I have to be up at dawn tomorrow morning and I can hear this damn music all the way over there." He pointed into the distance, toward his home.

Angelica threw back a sip of her newly opened beer, and Noah had to force himself not to watch, to not think about what her throat would look like swallowing down something else. "Have to or want to?" she asked archly.

Noah clenched his jaw and bit back a nasty retort. He didn't know what it was about this woman, but she got under his skin in a way no one ever had before. She'd been in River Hill for going on six weeks now and each interaction they'd had—save a few—had been an exercise in extreme patience.

"I like waking up at dawn. And I *don't* like the idea of having to switch up my routine to accommodate your loud parties."

One of the guys snickered, but when Noah shot him a glare, he immediately dropped his eyes to the fire and poked at it with a long stick. Meanwhile, Angelica glanced around the circle, taking in her companions before letting out a throaty laugh. "He thinks this is a party, gentlemen."

The guy closest to Angelica smirked and, with his eyes trained on Noah in a challenging stare, shook his head slowly. He knew that look. This guy thought Noah, with his flannel and his truck, was a stupid country yokel who he could talk down to. The mistaken impression didn't bother Noah. He loved River Hill and wasn't ashamed to call this place home. What he disliked, however, was the automatic dismissal, the snide, judgmental sneer the man had adopted. It was a sneer he knew well, having grown up surrounded by men and women who were equally as disapproving as this guy.

Noah raised his chin in defiance. "You got a problem?"

The two men stared at each other for several long, tense seconds before Angelica's tinkling laughter brought Noah back to himself. He didn't consider himself one of those aggressive alpha males that had to prove his manhood and virility in some ingrained evolutionary stand-off when he encountered another male skulking around his woman—

Wait, what? His woman?

In the blink of an eye, Noah understood exactly why he was standing there, his chest puffed out like some kind of avenging peacock. Sure, he and Angelica had gotten off on the wrong foot, but since she'd taken possession of the house, she'd been perfectly pleasant—exasperating, but charming. And he'd always, from the very second they'd met, thought she was the most stunning woman he'd ever laid eyes on. Noah was any number of things, but stupid wasn't one of them. As a winemaker, he knew a little something about scientific reactions … and right now he felt like an absolute fool for not having put two and two together sooner. This wasn't hate; it was chemistry. He didn't dislike Angelica. He might even like her—a lot. Unfortunately, what he *didn't* like was the idea that she might not like him back—that she might be fucking one of these guys instead of him.

Calm your goddamned horses, Noah thought. *No one said anything about fucking her.*

Chemistry wasn't the only subject Noah had

studied in college. He also knew a thing or two about biology, and he recognized these primal urges were something that had been hardwired into his DNA eons ago. He could give in to them and act like an asshole caveman by dragging Angelica off by her hair, or he could let all his culture and breeding and years of etiquette classes and social charm do the job for him.

Blinking away from the other man, Noah's eyes darted to Angelica and found her staring at him with an amused gleam.

"You were saying?" she asked, taking another swallow of her beer.

Noah cleared his throat. "I was saying the music was loud and I was trying to sleep. Can I convince you to turn it down a few notches? I don't have to get up early in the morning, but I like to." Casting bait he knew Angelica couldn't ignore, Noah added, "And Molly will be expecting her morning tromp through the woods."

"Oh yeah?" she asked, her interest mounting.

"Yup," he answered, shoving his hands deep into the pockets of his jeans. She might not have demonstrated much interest in *him* over the last several weeks, but Angelica was engaged in a full-fledged love affair with his dog. "Three mornings a week we head out to Armstrong Redwoods State Park before the day-trippers descend on the trails. You been?"

Angelica shook her head. "I've never heard of it."

"Oh yeah? You've seen *The Empire Strikes Back* though, right?"

One of the guys snorted. "Dude, we work in Hollywood. Of course we've seen it."

Ignoring the interloper, Noah's eyes stayed trained on Angelica. "That's Endor."

Angelica's face lit with recognition and she let out another tinkling laugh. "Oh my god! I know everyone hates the ewoks—"

"—Not as much as Jar Jar Binks," Noah reminded her.

She shook her head and chuckled. "No, not as much as Jar Jar Binks. But I *love* the ewoks; they're my favorite. They're so cute and cuddly and … diabolical." She leaned forward, her eyes gleaming with mischief.

Cute, cuddly, and diabolical—three words Noah might use to describe Angelica too. He laughed, and she raised an eyebrow at him, almost as if she could tell exactly what he'd been thinking.

Then she tilted her bottle to an empty stump next to her. "Why don't you sit for a few minutes and we can debate the sheer idiocy of Padmé falling for Anakin."

Noah hadn't been lying. He really wanted to get some sleep, but now that he'd given a name to these confusing feelings for Angelica, he also really wanted to explore them … so he sat. For the next several minutes, they chatted about their favorite moments from the *Star Wars* franchise, with Angelica's friends butting in left and right to offer their take on something Noah couldn't have cared less about. They were having an A and B conversation, and he really wished the others would C their fucking way out of it … but of course he wasn't about to say that. No, Noah hoped when he and Angelica continued to talk animatedly amongst themselves her guests would get a fucking clue and leave. They'd monopolized her conversation enough for one night—it was Noah's turn to have her attention, and he wanted it all for himself.

Eventually, Roger—a cameraman, Noah had learned, and obviously the smartest of the bunch—slapped his palms down onto his knees and stood. Stretching his back, he said, "We've got an early morning so we're going to head back to the hotel." One by one his companions rose and tossed their empty bottles into the garbage. Before they left, he turned to Angelica. "See you at nine then?"

She set her beer on the ground and shook Roger's hand. "Looking forward to it. I can't wait to start filming."

The six men climbed into three cars and pulled away, their rear brake lights flashing in the dark. And then it was just Noah and Angelica, alone, with nothing but the night sky twinkling overhead and the fire casting a warm glow over her face. A face Noah couldn't stop staring at. And because of that, he realized she suddenly looked guilty.

"Filming?" he asked, recalling what the other man had said.

She fidgeted, wiping her hands back and forth along her thighs, as she stared down into the flames. Eventually, her eyes flicked to his. "I didn't mention it?"

"Since I don't know what 'it' is, I couldn't say. Are

you doing another movie?" He poked at the fire with a long, coal-tipped branch.

Noah found the idea surprising. Over the last several weeks, they'd chatted here and there about the movies she'd been in and he'd always gotten the sense that Angelica *hated* Hollywood. He could tell she loved acting—the craft of it, inhabiting the characters she portrayed and becoming them, plus the sheer mechanical work of being on camera—but he was sure she could definitely do without the ass kissing and politics that went with it.

"Not exactly." She stood and grabbed a nearby pitcher, tossing water over the flames to put them out.

Noah jumped back in surprise when the wood hissed, and ash erupted in a steaming volcano. "Shit." With Angelica's retreating form several feet away now, he jogged to catch up, swiping white flecks from his torso and thighs.

With a tug on the weathered screen door, Angelica stepped into the mudroom and Noah followed. She hadn't invited him inside, but she hadn't said "goodnight" yet either, so he assumed her sudden departure smack in the middle of their conversation came with an open invitation for him to join her.

"Wait up." A few seconds later, he found her standing at the old, chipped farmhouse sink, idly rubbing her thumb over one of the black grooves in the porcelain, her eyes staring at the blackness outside. Stepping to her side, Noah asked, "Hey, what was that all about?"

Angelica flinched, and he wondered if she'd even heard him come in, heard him calling after her. He'd only known her a short while, but Noah had never seen her like this. Had he said or done something wrong? He wracked his brain to try and remember what it could have been and came up blank. They'd discussed *Star Wars*, her favorite films, his favorite TV shows, and then her friends had called it a night. Had it been something one of *them* had said? Admittedly, Noah hadn't been paying too much attention to the other men—he only had eyes and ears for Angelica now that he'd realized his annoyance with her stemmed not from hatred, but instead an intense, combustible attraction—but he didn't think that was it either.

"Hey, what happened back there?" he asked, laying a tentative hand on the soft, warm skin of her forearm.

Angelica dragged her eyes to his. Their gazes held for a few expectant heartbeats and then she sighed and turned to rest her hip against the counter. "I've been dreading this conversation all week," she said. "And especially with you being so nice all of a sudden."

"Hey," Noah replied with mock surprise and a cheeky grin. "I can be nice."

Angelica smiled back, her heart-shaped lips hitching up, but it didn't reach her eyes. "Not to me. You merely tolerate me."

Noah gripped the back of his neck and dropped his eyes. Flicking them back up, he said, "I think we can both agree we didn't meet under the most auspicious of situations."

"No, I know that, but I also apologized profusely and tried to do what I could to make it right. I thought you were excited about the land back there." She nodded toward the back of the house.

Noah dropped his hand and shoved them both in the pocket of his jeans. "I am. Really."

"Then why the sour face and bad attitude whenever our paths cross? One time I actually smelled my armpits because I was sure that I stunk." She cracked another small smile and Noah looked away guiltily.

He'd known he was being a dick to her but had felt justified in his behavior, even after they'd signed their contract. After all, it hadn't contained a provision that said he had to make nice with his nemesis.

Except ... Angelica *wasn't* his nemesis. She was a beautiful woman who Noah found mildly exasperating. One he very much wanted to kiss. All the damn time.

He wasn't a player—he left the womanizing to Sean now that he'd moved home—but he'd never been dumbfounded by a woman either, not the way he was with Angelica. It was like she'd twisted him inside out, and everything he thought he'd ever known about the fairer sex had been turned on its head.

Which was why he dragged his hands from his pockets and took a step closer, bringing him within inches of that delectable body of hers. Why he stroked the pad of his finger softly down the side of her face until he reached her jaw. He raised her chin until their eyes met and held, the black of Angelica's pupils bleeding into the deep blue of her irises as her chest rose and fell with labored breaths.

"You don't stink," Noah whispered as his head fell forward. "But I'd very much like to find out what you taste like."

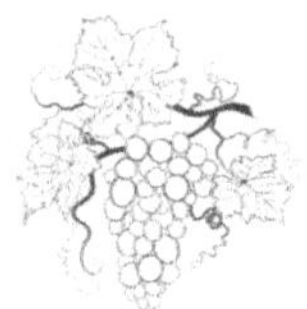

CHAPTER SIX

*H*e was kissing her. He was kissing her, and Angelica couldn't have pulled away if she'd wanted to. And god help her, she did *not* want to.

As his lips drifted to hers, she felt the pull between them like a physical force. His long fingers slid around her jawline, angling her head to meet his exploring lips. Her hands crept up to his shoulders without conscious thought, and her mouth opened under his to let their tongues slide against each other, tangling in a building frenzy.

Oh, god. This was Noah. Prickly, grumpy Noah, who admittedly had the finest body she'd ever seen and a chin you could light matches off of. They'd spent six weeks sniping at each other over every little thing. She'd thought he hated her. Apparently, his feelings were … something else.

She let her body move fully against his, feeling the edge of the countertop press into her back as an equally hard ridge in his jeans pressed against her front.

He made a sound, low in his throat, and the hand that wasn't at her neck slid down her body agonizingly slow until it reached her ass. His big hands fit all the way around her curves. *What else did he have that was big?* she wondered, moaning against his lips while his fingers flicked the edge of her t-shirt up. As they crept toward the waistline of her jeans, her body hummed with electricity.

Wait. They shouldn't be doing this.

Angelica pulled her hands from around his neck, put them on his shoulders, and pushed. "Wait. Noah." The effort to unseal her lips from his and speak was one of the hardest things she'd ever done. She felt the coolness of the air between them like someone had slapped her in the mouth with a heavy bag of ice cubes.

"Um. What?" He leaned away, looking as dazed as she felt.

They had a contract. She didn't sleep with people she did business with. And she still had to tell him about the crew. She and Jai had hammered out the details with the network over the last month; filming and construction would start in earnest tomorrow.

The camera crew had been over to survey the layout of the house all day. A few beers with the guys she'd be spending the next few months in close quarters with had seemed like a great icebreaker until Noah had showed up. And started kissing her.

She rested her forehead against his broad chest,

inhaling his clean, sharp scent and trying to ignore his fingers creeping back up under her shirt. "I need to talk to you," she said, and his fingers paused, then slid reluctantly back down, dragging sparks along her sensitive skin. She shivered, and he pressed against her, sliding his erection along her thigh before putting his hands at her waist and stepping back a fraction of an inch.

"About what?" He kissed her forehead when she raised her head. "If it's condoms, I'm packing, I promise."

She snorted. "How thoughtful of you."

He had the grace to look embarrassed. "I didn't plan—"

"I know you didn't." And she did, because Noah wasn't like that. And come to think of it, neither was she. Everything about what they were doing was so out of character for her it wasn't even funny.

But that's not what she needed to discuss with him. Any talk of sex could wait. Right now, she needed to be straight with him, and hope the tentative friendship they'd managed to carve out wouldn't be negatively impacted by her professional endeavors too badly. The truth was, Noah wasn't going to like what she had to tell him, and she didn't relish the idea of going back to the grumpy version of Noah now that she'd had a taste of Sexy Noah.

"It's not that," she said, setting her palm to her forehead and breathing out a sigh. "I've been meaning to tell you about this." She just hadn't been able to bring herself to do it, not when he'd been practically pleasant once or twice.

And now—well, now it was too late, and she had to put the genie back into the bottle. The hard, chiseled, extremely attractive genie who still had his hands on her, sending energy short-circuiting through her body and making her short of breath.

"About what?" His eyes were starting to clear, the haze of attraction retreating into his customary frown.

"The filming."

"What filming?"

She stepped out from between his arms, and he folded them as he watched her turn and fiddle with the coffee mugs in the drying rack next to the sink. She could feel his eyes boring into her shoulder blades. "I've signed on with Renovation Network Television to let them film my project." There was silence from the looming presence behind her, so she soldiered on. "The crew will be on site for at least the next eight weeks, filming me and my construction crews as we do the renovation of this place."

"You're doing a *reality series*?"

"It's not like I'm a Kardashian, Noah! It's a home renovation show."

"Let me get this straight. You're going to be bringing construction crews *and* film crews around here at all hours of the day and night?"

"I mean, it's not going to be at all hours—"

"Because you have such a great history of communicating with contractors." His voice dripped with sarcasm.

That was too much. She whipped around and glared at him. "Are you seriously bringing that up *again?*"

"It happened, didn't it?"

"And I made amends, Noah! You signed a damned contract!" She shoved her finger in his chest, glad of the reminder why she didn't mix business with pleasure. "You were just telling me five minutes ago that you're excited to start planting that hillside."

"I am. I would just prefer not to be on camera while doing it," he bit out.

"Nobody asked you to be on camera!"

Not that he wouldn't look good, of course. She lost herself for a brief second in a fantasy of watching him on a giant movie screen, twenty feet tall.

"How the hell am I supposed to get any work done if you've got those jerks crawling all over the place?" The fantasy version of Noah on her mental movie screen scowled at her, and she jerked back to reality.

"They're filming me, not you. They'll be all over the house and primary grounds. I'll make sure they know to stay out of your way."

He rolled his eyes. "I'm sure."

"If it's such a big deal, I'll have them sign contracts," she returned. "I hear you're pretty into that."

"Please. Like you Hollywood types have any interest in doing what you're told." There was dead silence for a moment as they both registered what he'd said. He raised his eyes to hers, and she couldn't interpret the expression in them. "I—"

"—I think you should go," she said as evenly as she could manage.

So much for Sexy Noah.

He pivoted without a word, and the screen door slammed behind him when he walked out.

Well. That had gone just about as well as she'd expected.

The next day, Angelica woke up both aroused and infuriated. Damn Noah Bradstone, anyway. She flung the covers away and shrugged into a tank top and stretchy, soft yoga pants. The camera crew wouldn't be here for at least another two hours, so she had plenty of time before she had to strap herself into a real bra. Coffee was a much more urgent requirement.

She padded into the kitchen and bit the inside of her cheek as she passed the counter where he'd pressed into her last night. Her lips still felt soft, and she swore she could still taste him. She shook her head.

Best get the coffee and stop your fantasizing.

Angelica slammed beans into her grinder, then the grounds into her French press, gritting her teeth as she remembered each and every second of last night—both the good ones *and* the bad. It was probably just as well that he'd revealed what he really thought about "Hollywood types" since she'd been in danger of breaking her personal rules for a minute there.

Coffee made, she sat down at the island with her laptop. Forget Noah, she had work to do. She tabbed to the window that contained the renovation checklist she kept stored in the cloud and began editing her timeline. An hour and a half later, she heard the rumble of wheels on the drive.

"Shit!" she shrieked, racing up the stairs to her bedroom.

No sports bra had ever been taken off as quickly as Angelica's was just now. It wasn't often these days that she changed undergarments twice in the span of a couple of hours, but there was no way she wanted the people she'd be working with to see the flattened uni-blob her comfy old racerback turned her breasts into. It was practical, and good for sitting around the house, but it definitely wasn't sexy, and it certainly didn't make her look camera-ready. Next, she switched the tank top she'd been wearing for a tee with a picture of Scooby Doo and Shaggy on it, and the yoga pants for baggy boyfriend jeans with a strategically placed hole in the knee. Her hair could stay in a ponytail; Roger had said they'd have a beauty crew in tow when they arrived. Finally, she tucked her socks into her back pocket and scurried for the front door.

"Ready?" Roger asked. He was a muscular man in his thirties with windswept, dark brown hair and dimples hidden under the scruff of a painstakingly maintained ten o'clock shadow.

Not that he was a vain man, but sometimes Angelica wondered if Roger Mewes didn't have a little extra help in that regard. The whiskers lining his jaw were just too damn perfect to be natural. She also thought he might visit a tanning salon once a week. It was sunny in California, but no one could maintain the sort of tan he sported with the hours he worked indoors. Suddenly, she couldn't help but compare it to Noah's California casual style, flannel shirt and real scruff included. Unfortunately for him, poor Roger just didn't stack up.

"Yep. Come on in," she said, stepping aside to welcome them all into her home, shambles though it may be.

As the crew tromped by her to set up their stationary equipment on the folding tables she'd stuck in the formal living room, she sat on the staircase to put her socks on.

"Ang?" The soft voice was familiar, and Angelica looked up in surprise.

"Leah! Nobody told me they'd talked you into this project!" She jumped up to hug the petite woman standing between two huge plastic cases marked MAKEUP in permanent black marker.

Leah Strange hugged her back. "I needed a change of pace, so it wasn't too hard to convince me." Her signature red hair had been chopped decisively into a pixie cut, just as flattering as the angled bob she'd sported the last time Angelica had seen her. Everything looked good on Leah. Perfect eyebrows over big brown eyes in skin that didn't need the products she carried? Angelica had once heard another actress demand, "Just make me look like *you!*" in the makeup chair.

She tightened her arms around the smaller woman, then released her. "Please tell me you haven't had another breakup."

"Would if I could," the other woman said cheerfully, a hint of her Southern accent still remaining. "But my Daddy says I'm descended from George Washington, so I don't lie."

Angelica laughed. Leah had been an assistant on the hair and makeup team for her first movie, and they'd formed an easy bond. They didn't see each all that often, but Angelica had always been delighted on the rare occasions she'd slipped into a makeup chair and found Leah standing behind it.

"I'm surprised to find you doing TV work," she said, picking up one of the makeup cases and heading to the kitchen. "Best light in here, probably."

"Rumors are flyin', honey, and I wanted to be in on the ground floor." Leah's tinkling laugh had always reminded Angelica of some kind of fairy. "Pun intended."

"Rumors?"

"Anytime a celebrity does one of these renovation shows, there are questions, Ang."

Angelica winced. "I wouldn't call myself a celebrity."

"Vanilla Ice did it."

"And I'm definitely *not* Vanilla Ice."

"Mmm. Thank goodness. I don't think his highlights would look good on you." Leah unsnapped the metal locks and flipped each case's lid open with the practiced ease of a professional. "I called Jai."

"Of course you did."

"He told me you were making major changes."

"Of course he did."

"And, needing a break as I was, I made a few calls, and called in a few favors."

Angelica snorted. Leah was at the top of her game, so she must really have wanted a break from L.A. Otherwise, there was no explanation why the talented woman had been willing to take what must have been a substantial pay cut. The RenoTV folks had probably been panting to hire her. It was a coup for them, but for her friend? Well, something must be up.

"Leah … is everything okay?"

"Sit." Leah pushed Angelica down onto the stool next to the island. "Everything's fine. Stop frowning, I need to look at your face," she said, quickly flicking through the cases, tubes, and tins in her supplies, pulling a few things out as she went.

"But—"

"You're not the only one who wants a change, honey." Leah smoothed the skin around Angelica's eyebrows with steady fingers, then frowned. "What's this?" She traced around the edges of Angelica's lips, and her eyebrows flew up. "Angelica!"

"What?" Angelica tugged her head away from her friend's too-knowing gaze.

"Nobody told me I'd be covering up stubble tracks." Leah smirked. "Who haven't I met?"

"Nobody."

"Somebody's been awfully close to your face for a nobody. Fresh, too." Leah reached into her case for a concealer. "Can't lie to your makeup girl. Last night? Rog said something—"

"I'm not surprised." Angelica rolled her eyes. "He was ready to have a pissing contest right then and there."

"Who?"

"Both of them."

"Rog and …?" Leah let the words trail off on a note of inquiry.

Angelica gave in with a sigh. "You'll meet him soon enough. I'm sure he'll come storming in here to yell at us before too long."

"Sounds like a peach. What's this paragon's name?"

"Noah Bradstone. He lives next door." Angelica waved a hand in the direction of Noah's property.

"And he is?" Leah was a master interrogator, apparently.

"Infuriating, grumpy. Ridiculously attractive. Off limits."

"To you, or to me?"

Angelica bit back the flow of unexpected jealousy. "Me. But I wouldn't recommend him for you, either. He doesn't have a high opinion of people from Hollywood. Or people in general, as far as I can tell."

Leah grinned. "I look forward to meeting him." She leaned near, brush in hand. "Close your eyes."

Angelica closed her eyes obediently and felt the expert application of liner and shadow happening. "What about Roger?"

"What about him?"

"Don't act innocent with me. I remember when you dated."

"That was years ago, Angelica."

"Not that long."

"At least four boyfriends ago, which is basically an eternity."

"Normal people don't measure time by relationships, Leah."

Leah sniffed. "Normal is overrated. Hair next."

Angelica opened her eyes. "Up or down?"

"Your hair, or my relationships?"

"My hair, you weirdo."

Leah glanced down at a clipboard glued into the lid of her makeup case. "Says we're doing preliminary walkthrough shots today, so let's go for fabulous instead of feisty."

"The glamorous celebrity leads you through a tour of her home?"

Leah laughed. "You got it." She handed Angelica a sparkling hair pin. "Hold that, I'll do a quick blowout."

One quick spray and a noisy blowout later, Angelica looked in the mirror Leah held in front of her face. "You do good work, kid."

"Call me kid and I'll knock your kneecaps out," Leah said sweetly.

"Only because that's all you can reach."

"Keep it up, Boobs McGrath. I'm the one making you look good today."

"You're right, I'm sorry." Angelica grinned at her friend. "Are we ready?"

Leah nodded. "I'll be on hand for touch-ups."

"Sounds good. Time to go find Roger and remind him of your everlasting love."

"You're going to look like a raccoon tomorrow."

"I'll fit right in then." She grinned impishly. "Have you been out to the shed yet?"

Leah followed her out of the kitchen, running a finger down the chair rail in the foyer and making a face when it came away covered in dust. "You know this place is a dump, right?"

"I do, but it's my dump," Angelica said with a firm nod. "And it's going to be gorgeous. What you just did to my face?" She circled her head with her finger and waited for Leah's nod. "I'm going to do that to this house."

"You're going to need a lot of concealer."

"We call it drywall," Angelica said with a grin. "And there's a truckload being delivered tomorrow."

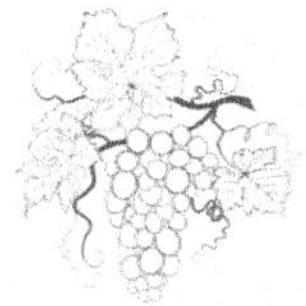

CHAPTER SEVEN

Hooking his sunglasses onto the neck of his faded gray t-shirt, Noah reached for the door to The Hollow Bean, his favorite coffee shop in River Hill, and stepped over the threshold. He stopped dead in his tracks. Because there she was. Angelica Travis: his greatest desire and the biggest nemesis, all wrapped up in one mouth-watering package.

Up until the other night things had been going well between them. So well, in fact, that he couldn't get the taste of her off his lips, couldn't stop thinking about what the rest of her would taste like, too. But damn it if she wasn't the most infuriating woman he'd ever met. As he'd gotten to know her better, one of the things he appreciated most was that she'd willingly walked away from a life in Hollywood to pursue her dream of opening and running a B&B. He'd been impressed by her fortitude in the face of uncertainty, and by her complete faith in her ability to succeed in this new venture. She'd reminded him a bit of himself in that regard, if he was being honest.

But now that she'd told him about the TV show she'd be starring in, he had to wonder if she had meant all the things she'd told him, or if she'd only said what she thought he wanted to hear. She was an actress, after all, and delivering scripted lines was her specialty.

What other bullshit might she have fed me?

For a fleeting second Noah considered turning around and walking out, but this was *his* town, and he refused to be chased out of all his favorite haunts just because *she* was there. Besides, River Hill was a small community; he'd better get used to running into her whenever he stepped foot in town.

He ran a hand through his hair, noted that it was getting overly long, and stepped into line behind her. Even though ogling a woman in public wasn't the gentlemanly thing to do, he couldn't stop his eyes from falling to Angelica's ass encased in soft, well-worn denim. Now that he knew how that sensuous flesh filled out his palms, he didn't think he'd ever be able to keep from staring. Which was a problem since he probably wouldn't get a chance to repeat the experience anytime soon.

Unless ...

Noah knew he'd reacted harshly, but that was only because he'd been disappointed. The truth was, he'd grown to *like* Angelica these past few weeks. He'd found her exasperating at times, sure, but what women wasn't? But now that he'd learned where her priorities lay, he'd gained a bit of clarity where his sexy neighbor was concerned. The more he thought about it, the more he wondered if this show wasn't a good thing after all. Somebody who was committed to a TV show wouldn't be looking for a commitment from him, and that sounded … well, perfect actually.

Not to mention, their chemistry was off-the-charts explosive, and if they didn't do something about it soon, Noah wasn't sure either of them would survive the combustion. He definitely wasn't in the market for a relationship—and now he suspected Angelica wasn't either—but that didn't mean they couldn't enjoy each other. Specifically, each other's bodies. They just needed to keep things nice and friendly between them without stepping over the line.

But first, he'd have to eat crow.

He stepped closer and cleared his throat, causing Angelica to swing her head around to investigate the noise. When her eyes landed on him, her pupils flared but then her gaze turned flinty. "Oh, it's you."

"Yup, it's me," he said, rocking back on his heels. "Who were you expecting?"

"Go away." Angelica faced forward, giving him her back.

"Sorry, no can do."

Noah couldn't see her face, but he'd bet she was speaking through gritted teeth when she said, "Isn't there another coffee shop you could go to?"

He laughed and shook his head. *Who the heck did this woman think she was?* "You're kidding, right?" The

Hollow Bean was River Hill's only coffee shop. Which was why the line was always so damn long.

Angelica peered at him over her shoulder. "Does this look like the face of a woman who's joking?"

Noah took a few moments to study said woman. *Damn.* Just looking at Angelica caused his temperature to spike and his dick to swell. Which reminded him what he needed to do if he was going to get to touch her again. "I wanted to apologize for my behavior the other night."

Angelica raised an eyebrow, and he noticed that since he'd last seen her last, they'd been groomed into perfectly sculpted arches. His gaze roved over her face, taking in other changes in her appearance. The adorable freckles that dotted the bridge of her nose had been masked by a heavy layer of makeup, and her eyes were dusted with a shimmery shadow that reminded him of the burnished hillside behind his house during the height of summer.

"What happened to your face?" he blurted. When Angelica winced, he realized how his words had sounded. "Shit, I didn't mean for it to come out like that." He scrubbed a frustrated hand over his jaw. He had never been very good at apologizing. "I just meant, your face looks different."

"It's called makeup." She turned her head away, giving him her profile.

"I know what it is." He rolled his eyes. "What I mean to say is, *why* are you wearing makeup?"

Not that he thought she looked bad—because she

didn't, she looked fucking beautiful—but he'd gotten used to seeing her all fresh-faced and relaxed, not this primped and polished version of her. It reminded him of the women his mother was always trying to set him up with.

"Everyone wears makeup on TV." Her tone was excessively patient, her voice rising an octave as if explaining a very simple idea to a very simple person.

"Yeah, but you don't need it," Noah said as he edged out from behind her to eye her from the side and make room for the growing line.

When the customer at the front of the line paid and moved aside to wait for his order, they both took a step forward, and Angelica lifted her face to study the chalkboard menu, ignoring Noah's words.

He waited, but when she *continued* ignoring him, Noah plowed on. "Because you're beautiful without it."

Angelica's lips hitched up in a small, shy smile that she quickly fought to control, but it was too late—he'd seen it, and he'd be damned if he wasn't going to build on that tiny bit of progress. Stepping close enough to smell her light, floral scent, he traced the line of her collarbone with his finger. "I always think you're beautiful."

He watched with satisfaction as her skin turned a becoming shade of pink, starting somewhere below the neckline of her shirt and moving up to color her cheeks. But before he could lean forward and whisper in her ear that he'd bet good money she looked best with nothing on at all, it was her turn to step forward and place her order.

As she asked the barista for a triple cappuccino, Noah pulled his wallet from his back pocket. "Make that two," he said, handing over a ten-dollar bill.

"I can pay for my own coffee, Noah."

"I know. But it's the least I can do to make up for the other night."

Angelica's cheeks colored again, and Noah's dick stirred with the memory of her curves pressed up against his hard body. Why couldn't she have waited to tell him about the show until after they'd fucked? He'd probably still have been angry, but this way, he'd left both angry *and* sexually frustrated.

"There's no need," Angelica responded, interrupting his wayward thoughts.

She could argue all she liked, but he was buying her goddamned coffee. With a fixed stare, he accepted his change from the barista. "Too late. I win."

Angelica stepped aside to wait for her order. "Is that what this is about? Winning?"

Noah stared at her in bewilderment. "What?"

"This thing between you and me," she answered, rolling her hand between them. "You always have to have the upper hand."

"That's not true," he protested, as an uncomfortable sensation of dismay grew in his chest. The thing was, Angelica wasn't the first woman who'd accused him of something like that. He was competitive—he knew that

—but he didn't think it was as bad as she was making it out to be.

"It is," she said firmly. "The vines, the tacos, the music, the coffee. You always have to be right, always have to come in first."

He blinked long and slow and inhaled a frustrated breath. He didn't want to admit that she was right but … she wasn't wrong, either. He opened his eyes. "What can I say or do to make things right between us? I'm tired of fighting with you."

She studied him for a few brief moments while his heart hammered in his chest. He didn't know why, but suddenly he was very worried about how she'd answer. Suddenly he had this overwhelming fear that she'd say there was *nothing* he could do. And that would be bad. Very, very bad. Because as much as she infuriated him, she also intrigued him.

Peering up at him, Angelica's mouth lifted into a smile she didn't try to hide this time. "Tell you what. I've smelled you barbecuing a few times and I *know* you have good wine at your place. How about you invite me over, ply me with steak and alcohol, and we can start over?"

Noah smiled at her offer of a truce and tried not to think what else he'd like to ply her with. "I'd planned on cooking up some ribeyes tonight. You free?"

She grabbed their coffees off the counter and passed his cup to him. "Six o'clock work?"

Quickly, Noah calculated everything he still had to

do that day, including cleaning up his house and making sure his bed was made with fresh sheets and blankets. He had a meeting down in Santa Rosa later that afternoon and with rush hour traffic, he didn't think he'd be back until well after dark. "Can we make it 7:30?" he asked.

Angelica pursed her lips and lifted her eyes to the ceiling. "I have an early call time tomorrow but if you think you can wine and dine me by ten, that should be fine."

"What time?"

"Um, ten?" Angelica asked, clearly confused by his question.

"No, I mean what time do you need to be up tomorrow?"

"We start filming at 7 a.m., which means I have to be in the makeup chair by six. *That* means I need to be up by five." She contorted her face into a look of mock horror and he laughed.

"Perfect. Me too."

Again, Noah realized too late how his words had sounded. *He* wasn't going to be in a makeup chair. "I just meant that I have to be up early too, so I won't keep you up too late."

She smirked, and he chuckled in response. "I swear I'm not usually this bad." His tongue usually got him into trouble in very different, more pleasurable ways.

"I don't know," she said, hitching her purse higher on her shoulder as they moved through the tables and out the door. "You seem to find yourself saying things you don't mean to an awful lot."

"Only around you," Noah admitted. She stopped and raised a disbelieving eyebrow. "I'm serious, ask anyone."

"Sure." She snickered as they reached her car.

Noah shook his head and took a sip of his coffee. "So, seven thirty then?"

Angelica dropped down into the seat of her BMW. "It's a date." She winked at him..

Noah closed the door of her car and flashed her a rueful smile as she started the ignition. When she rolled down the window, he said, "You're trouble. You know that, right?"

Her responding smile made him bite back a startled gasp as her whole face lit with happiness. She'd smiled at him before, but this was the first time he could recall her looking so ... so ... enchanting was the only word he could think of to adequately describe her now.

"I *do* know." She put her car into reverse and backed it up. When she was a few feet away, she leaned out the window. "My parents have been telling me that since I was five. The sooner you accept it, the easier things will be." She winked again, threw her car into drive, and pulled away.

Noah watched her tail lights until she reached the stop sign at the intersection, then shook his head and climbed into his truck with a smile glued to his face. Angelica Travis might infuriate him, but she also made him laugh like no woman had in a very long time. And if he wasn't careful, those two things could prove dangerous.

CHAPTER EIGHT

I definitely can't show up to dinner like this. Angelica stared down at her dust-covered and paint-spattered jeans in dismay. She and the crew had spent the afternoon patching up drywall and painting one of the guest bedrooms—and filming the whole thing, of course. Roger had taken particular delight in the gob of spackle that had landed in her hair when she'd attempted to reach a little too high. She'd heard the lens zooming in from across the room.

With a bit more cleaning, she'd have at least one room ready, which would satisfy her parents. Her mother had agreed to appear on the show, helping Angelica make design decisions and hang artwork. Meanwhile, her father was planning on installing some kind of bookkeeping software on her computer. Off camera, or so he said. She expected to see him pulled into some kind of interview about five minutes after

Leah and Roger got their hands on him. Assuming those two stopped avoiding each other, anyway.

Angelica stripped, chuckling as she thought about her friend's adamant denials of anything ever happening again with the cameraman. If they weren't sleeping together within a week, she'd eat her spackle knife.

A quick shower did a lot for the dust and most of the paint, but to Angelica's consternation, she'd had to snip out a small chunk of hair with a pair of rusted kitchen shears to get the last of the dried spackle out. Leah was going to kill her.

Now, she stood naked in front of the old, mottled mirror in her bathroom. Sliding her hands down along her hips, she tried not to think about Noah's hands doing the same. Even when he wasn't with her, that man was a major distraction. While she couldn't quit picturing all the things she wanted him to do to her, she was absolutely, one hundred percent positive he wasn't looking for something serious.

Not that she was, either. She needed to stay focused on her renovation so she could make this place a success.

Angelica's hands slipped lower and she met her own heavy-lidded gaze in the mirror. There was nothing stopping them from being friends, though. Maybe even friends with benefits. She wondered if he was thinking the same thing. He'd been positively charming today. It was a side of him she hadn't expected.

Before she could become too distracted, she shook her head and pushed all those tantalizing thoughts away. It was after seven. She needed to get herself dressed and over to Noah's. If nothing else, she was pretty sure a really good steak was in her future.

_____

He answered the door in a sage green tee that was either vintage-wash or truly vintage, because it clung to his muscles in a way that emphasized the softness of the material and the body underneath. Angelica managed not to swallow her tongue, and walked inside when he gestured her in.

"Everything's just about ready," he said. "I was just waiting for you to get here to toss the steaks on the grill."

She followed him down the hallway to the kitchen, letting her eyes travel over him while his back was turned. That soft green fabric was caught up in the waistband of his jeans at the back, giving her a truly excellent view of his superior ass. She caught herself nodding in time as each cheek moved with his long strides.

"Sounds great," she said absently. She was pretty sure he'd been saying something about steak.

"You said pinot, right?"

"Hmm?" She drew her gaze up and realized that they were standing in his kitchen, a modern master-piece in cherry wood and granite, with a contrasting center island in dark gray, all sparklingly clean. Noah moved around the island, his hip skimming the edge of the countertop and held up a glass and a bottle.

"Pinot. As requested."

"Ooh, is it yours?" She came closer, intrigued.

He laughed. "Actually, no. But local, I promise." The wine had already been uncorked and resting, clearly. He picked up a glass and poured her a small sample with the practiced ease of a professional at work. No extra flourishes or swirls with Noah. She liked that about him, she realized. He wasn't flashy or pretentious; he was just himself. Occasionally grumpy, sometimes irritating, secretly charming, and dead sexy.

"Thanks." She took a sip and nodded. "It's good."

"Should go nicely with ribeye," he said. "And I stole a gratin from Max."

"Really? Doesn't he need it for his customers?" She couldn't imagine waltzing into a restaurant's kitchen and making off with a dish herself, but she could definitely picture Noah doing it.

"Nah. He feeds me occasionally, and I give him a damned good discount when he stocks his cellar."

"Scratching each other's backs, huh?"

He grinned at her. "You should see the pastry I stole from Sean's mom for dessert."

"Do you pay for anything?" She'd meant to sound disapproving, but it came out on a bubble of laughter.

He picked up a platter and angled it toward her. "Sure. Steak."

"Is that just because you don't know any cattle ranchers?"

"None. My social circles are really shallow," he said, shaking his head with mock sadness.

"Maybe you can network your way up the culinary ladder," she suggested. "Is there an online dating app for dudes who just want to trade food with each other?"

"If there isn't, there should be."

"Impress Your Date Dot Com?"

"That sounds more like a self-help site."

She chuckled. "Naming things isn't really my forte."

He nodded toward the door. "Come on. Grill's hot already."

She followed him outside and admired his deck. It was spacious, with both a table and a seating area with elegant, simple furniture. Clean lines were definitely Noah's style, she decided. He slid an oiled towel along the grill's grate and then flipped the steaks onto the hot iron like he was dealing cards. They gave a satisfying sizzle, and he nodded at them with what looked like affection. "Nice." Then he turned, and she found his focus back on her. "So, what are you going to name your place?"

"What?"

"Your B&B. Have you decided on a name?"

She took another sip of her wine. "Not really."

"Got any ideas?"

If she took any more sips of wine to avoid answering, she'd be drunk before the steaks were finished cooking. "Not good ones," she admitted with a grimace.

He grinned. "Well, now I *definitely* want to hear them."

"Of course you do," she said, rolling her eyes.

"Come on. Give me your best shot." He glanced back at the steaks and seemed to decide they weren't quite ready to flip yet. "Let's hear it."

She shrugged. "I don't know. I was thinking … like … The Butterfly?"

He stared at her. "You've either watched too many episodes of *Gilmore Girls* or you're a huge fan of Mariah Carey."

"I told you I'm bad at names."

"Give me another."

"Angelica's Place."

He roared with laughter. "No! You haven't seriously considered that."

"Until I realized it made it sound like I was opening a corner bar."

"Or a daycare center."

"Gee, thanks." She stuck out her tongue.

"Do you have more?"

"Not any worth sharing, apparently."

Still chuckling, he turned back to the steaks and flipped them. "You need a name coach."

"Are you offering?"

"Maybe. Here, hold this." He handed her a plate.

"There's no food on this."

"You're very observant."

She set her glass down to get a better grip on the plate. It was simple, plain white, just what she expected from Noah. She held it out as he poked the steaks with a finger to judge their doneness. "Medium rare, please," she instructed.

"Hmph." He pulled one of the steaks off the grill and slid it onto the plate for himself. "I suppose you don't like food to be moving when it gets to your plate."

"Not much, anyway. Not if I'm going to eat it."

"Well, I'm just glad you didn't order it well done. You would have had to leave."

"Perfectly understandable." She grinned at him.

They stood in companionable silence for another few moments until he judged her steak ready and pulled it off the grill. "Here, I'll take that," he said, reaching for the plate. "You get the door."

She skipped forward to open the door and he set the steaks down on the counter before rummaging in a drawer for a potholder. "Gratin's done, too. There's a salad in the fridge. Can you grab it for me?"

She moved around the other side of the island while he extracted the bubbling potatoes from the oven. Finding a simple, fresh salad in the fridge, she asked, "Did you pick this up at the farmers' market?"

"Mmm-hmm," he answered, setting the gratin on the counter. He pointed to an empty spot next to it, indicating she should put the salad there, and then turned to pull plates out of a cabinet. "Want to eat inside or outside?"

"Outside," she said. "Your deck is fabulous."

"Thanks. No fire pit or anything, but I like it."

"Well, if you're feeling desperate, you can always come over to my place," she offered. "To use the fire pit. Not to, like, burn it all down."

He laughed as he spooned potatoes onto their plates. "Thanks for clarifying."

They carried their meals outside to the table on the deck, and he refilled their glasses from the bottle of wine he'd brought with him.

"This all looks amazing," Angelica said, surveying the spread. She wasn't used to home cooking, to be honest. It wasn't a skill she'd developed herself, and she certainly hadn't met a lot of men in Southern California who bothered. "Thanks for doing this."

"Thanks for coming," he said, and raised his glass. "Toast to us."

"To us?"

"Friends, I hope," he said with a smile.

Angelica couldn't identify the feeling in the pit of her stomach as she clinked her glass against his. Disappointment? Frustrated lust? Hunger? "Friends," she said with a smile, hoping it didn't twist too much.

He leaned forward, and she caught her breath at the intensity that had suddenly sprung up in his eyes. "Were you thinking of something else?" he asked quietly.

"I—"

"Because I have to say, I was."

She blinked. "You … ah, you were?"

"Every time I see you," he confessed. "I keep

thinking about the other night. The good part, not the arguing."

"The good part," she breathed.

"It *was* good, wasn't it?"

Good was an understatement. Just remembering it made her want to leap into his lap, preferably without clothes on. But as far as she knew, neither of them were in the market for a relationship, and there was still the matter of her personal policy about dating business partners.

"I don't date anybody I've signed a contract with," she blurted.

He sat back and dipped his fork into his potatoes. "I wasn't … uh … necessarily talking about dating."

"I—oh."

"Listen. I like you," he said. "You're a pain in the ass sometimes, but I'd really like to explore what's going on between us."

"Flattering," she said dryly.

"You want flattery?" he asked with an imperious quirk of his eyebrow. "You and I both know that you're gorgeous, Angelica." He slid her a side-eyed glance that practically smoldered. "But I'd really like to see more, if you know what I mean."

She gulped. She *did* know what he meant, and the feeling was definitely mutual. But … "We agreed to an early night," she said reluctantly. "I can't reschedule my call time this late."

"Does that mean you're interested?"

She bit her tongue before answering. "I … yes. I'm

interested. Friends with benefits, so to speak. Just, maybe not tonight."

He ran his fingers through his hair and sighed. She could hear the frustration in his voice. "You're right, actually. I have to kick you out by ten."

She giggled. "Nice."

He pointed a finger at her, mock-sternly. "Don't get mouthy with me, woman." Then he grinned, and it was *very* clear where his thoughts were headed. "Not tonight, anyway."

She laughed. "We'll see. For tonight, steak will have to do." She sliced into hers and held up a bite in mock salute to him before she popped it into her mouth. His eyes followed her mouth as she chewed and swallowed, and the intensity in them made her entire body hot.

They finished dinner without much more mention of what was growing between them, although she knew she'd spent a little too much time carefully licking the cream sauce from the gratin off of her fork. At one point, she'd thought he might leap over the table. Instead, he'd retaliated over dessert, spending far too much time leaning over her shoulder as he served the pastry, and then using those long fingers of his to ease a bit of cream out of the center of his serving and into his mouth. She'd nearly fallen out of her chair.

And now it was ten o'clock, and neither of them were naked. A successful evening, by somebody's measure, she supposed, trying to remember that she'd be up far too early the next morning. And Leah would kill her if there were bags under her eyes. Or at least make several lewd comments.

Noah led her to the door, then drew her in close. She tilted her head up reflexively, and found his lips on hers in a soft, sweet kiss. He lingered, then pulled away and rested his forehead on hers. "What are you doing on Saturday?"

"Mmm." She enjoyed the press of his body, feeling every last ridge of muscle in his chest sliding up against her. "Nothing, really. The crew's off for the weekend. Just need to place some orders for tile."

"Okay. Put me on your calendar."

"Oh?"

"Yeah. Friendship day," he said.

She felt a jolt of what felt like disappointment. "Really?"

He raised his head and grinned down at her. "Hey. You'll like it. There's more to being friends with me than just jumping my bones, you know."

She couldn't resist. "I'll have to check with the guys at Frankie's to be sure."

He rolled his eyes with a grin. "I'm sure plenty of people have sex with Max and Sean, but I'm not one of them." He punctuated it with another kiss. "Dress in comfortable clothes. And sneakers." He pointed down at her feet, currently encased in her favorite heels. "None of those, much as I appreciate them." His hands slid down from her waist to cup her ass, and he pulled her tight to him for one last, lingering kiss and a suggestive hip thrust that pushed her back against the door. "Now get out."

She went, laughing. Leah was going to have a few smart ass things to say about stubble marks again, but this time, Angelica definitely had no regrets.

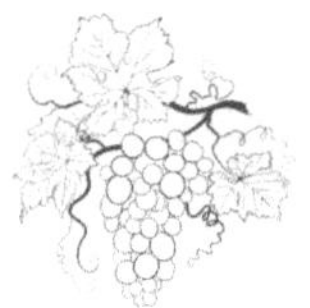

CHAPTER NINE

Noah pulled his truck up in front of Angelica's house, taking an extra moment before exiting to calm his nerves. He didn't know why his heart was racing or his belly was in knots. This was a simple date, nothing more. He'd been on hundreds of them. Although, if he was being honest with himself, lately he hadn't been dating so much as just periodically heading over to Naomi's place for dinner and a nice, uncomplicated fuck with someone who wouldn't expect a ring on her finger afterward.

Over the years, he'd gotten tired of trying to weed out who was genuinely interested in him versus who just wanted the Blackstone family name—not to mention access to its fortune. Naomi had rejected her own wealthy roots and didn't have any interest in either. She was sweet, uncomplicated, and utterly uninterested in anything but friendship with a few side benefits. But he hadn't even thought about Naomi since the second he'd started arguing with—and ogling —Angelica. He didn't think his old friend would particularly care, though.

His proposed arrangement with Angelica was virtually the same as the one he'd had with Naomi, but something about Angelica herself made it feel completely different. He legitimately liked spending time with her outside the bedroom. She affected him like no one else ever had. When he wasn't infuriated by her, he couldn't stop thinking about her … wondering what she was doing, how she was getting on with her remodel, what she'd think about a story he wanted to relay to her. And ever since that kiss? Well, his thoughts had included a whole lot more than talking, too.

Before his mind—and his dick—could run away with those thoughts, he exited the truck's cab, Molly trailing behind. When he reached Angelica's ramshackle front porch, she stepped outside to greet him, her face split in a luminescent smile that took his breath away. He had to physically stop and marvel at how this woman seemed to be lit from within by something pure and good.

From behind her back, Angelica produced two plain brown paper bags—one held aloft in each hand. "One turkey, one ham," she said, alternating which one she held higher.

"You didn't have to do that," he said, his feet propelling him forward. "I planned to feed you."

Angelica chewed on her lip and dropped the bags

back down to her sides. "Oh, well. I wasn't sure. You didn't say ..." She shrugged a freckled shoulder and looked away, almost as if she was embarrassed for having performed this thoughtful gesture.

Noah scowled, upset that his characteristically blunt speech had dimmed her smile. He sighed, and ran a hand through his hair, already mussed and sticking up in several directions, even though he'd tried to comb it into a semblance of something resembling a hairstyle. They were going to be spending a lot of time outdoors today, but he'd still wanted to look good for her. She was a stunningly beautiful woman, and his vanity required her to think he wasn't a chore to look at either. Noah knew he wasn't ugly, but he was a little rough around the edges and didn't typically spend a lot of time worrying about his appearance. For Angelica, he'd tried to make an effort.

The thing about her though was that her beauty was natural and effortless. With her hair pulled through a baseball cap to sway down her back in a long ponytail, the filtered morning sun dappled the skin around her neck, chest, and shoulders with shadows and light, and he didn't think he'd ever seen a more beautiful sight.

Unable to control himself, he took a few steps forward, eliminating the distance between them, and traced his fingers over a dancing leaf of light near her collarbone. "Hi," he said once he'd completed his traversal of her petal soft skin.

Angelica swallowed, and her eyes flicked between his. "Hi," she eventually breathed out.

"Thank you for the food. And before I forget, you look beautiful." Noah's gaze raked over her a second time in quiet appreciation.

She was dressed uber-casual today, in a plain white tank top and cutoff jean shorts that highlighted her toned, tanned thighs, but he wouldn't have wanted her any other way. Despite her former occupation as an actress, Angelica Travis seemed *real*. He'd spent years surrounded by women pretending to be someone they weren't, going under the knife to look like anyone but themselves. But with her slightly crooked front tooth and the fine laugh lines that fanned out from her eyes, he would guess Angelica had never once visited a plastic surgeon's office—not the way so many of the socialites his mother forcefully put in his path had already done, even though they were younger than he was.

She hiccuped a giggle and gripped her ponytail. "Thank you, but I'm calling bullshit. It turns out the plumber didn't get my showers fixed yesterday like he was supposed to, so this morning's ablutions were a bit on the perfunctory side." She frowned, pulled her hair in front of her nose, and sniffed. "I still smell like last night's steak."

Noah's lips hitched up in a small smile. "Ablutions?" Not the sort of vocabulary he'd expected a Hollywood princess to have. Or even a renovation queen. As usual, she was full of surprises.

Angelica pushed at his shoulder playfully. "Shut up. I read a lot of Regency romances and I love that word."

Noah smiled down at her, charmed to the bone, and then clicked his tongue to his dog. Obeying the unspoken command, she trotted over to the truck.

"Morning Molly!" Angelica called out as the dog stood at the tailgate, her wagging tail sending a cloud of dust into the air behind her.

With his hand on Angelica's back, Noah ushered her toward the truck. "According to the Google machine, you had a part in a Jane Austen movie?" he asked. It made more sense now that he knew of her love of the Regency era.

Before she could answer, he opened the truck's door and helped her inside. Then he did the same with his dog, before climbing in and starting the engine.

Angelica picked up where they'd left off. "Yeah, just a small part though. I played the bumbling sister." She shrugged and grimaced. "I wasn't really thrilled to take a role that made me look like such an idiot, but I'm a huge Austen fan and the chance to be in a movie based on one of her books was too good to pass up. A dream come true, really."

Taking the bumpy country road slow so as not to kick up too much dirt, Noah glanced her way. "Then I'm glad you did it. I'll have to watch it sometime."

She laughed. "No, please don't. Like I said, bumbling idiot."

In one quick look, he took her in from head to toe, loving every inch on display for him. "Bumbling, gorgeous idiot, I'm sure."

When Angelica's cheeks turned pink, he dragged his eyes back to the road and forced himself not to imagine what her whole body would look like blushing under the weight of his … adoration. He could picture, in mouth-watering detail, the flush of her skin as it heated from his touch.

She cleared her throat self-consciously, almost as if she could read his mind and see where his lustful thoughts had taken him. "So. What's on the agenda for Friendship Day?"

Right. Friendship day, he thought as he turned the truck down a long avenue lined with coastal redwoods. He flicked his eyes from the road to meet her's. "I was thinking we'd start with a quick walk through Endor, and then we'd head out to the coast for some BBQ oysters."

She clapped with delight and bounced in her seat. "You're taking me to the Ewoks!"

Noah chuckled. "Yeah. I figured you'd like that."

"Oh, I do." Her palms dropped to her thighs, calling attention to her attire. "But I'm not really dressed for a tromp through the woods."

Even though he was trying his damnedest not to ogle her, Angelica's words felt like an open invitation. With a sideways glance, he traced a path from her ankles to her thighs, and then skimmed his gaze up the rest of her body until their eyes met. Her lips were split in a sly smile of her own.

Yeah, she knows exactly what she's doing, he thought,

bringing his eyes back around to the road as they pulled up alongside the ranger station to pay the park entrance fee.

"Normally I'd do a longer, more difficult hike in the morning, but I didn't know what you'd be up for, so we're sticking to a wide, well-tended path I've seen toddlers handle with ease."

She laughed. "Are you calling me a toddler?"

"Far from it."

Less than ten minutes later, they strolled together under the canopy of the redwoods, pine needles crunching beneath their feet. Technically, Molly was supposed to be on a leash, but at this early hour the path was nearly deserted so Noah let her trot ahead, her tongue hanging out of her mouth as she explored the forest floor with her nose.

"It really is beautiful here," Angelica remarked, her head tipped back to take in the grandeur of the ancient trees. "Like a whole other world."

She was right, of course, but he was having a hard time seeing past her beauty. "Maybe the most beautiful," he murmured, his chest panging with a longing he wasn't used to feeling.

Angelica's face dropped forward and their eyes locked.

At the same time, they each took a step forward, and then another.

"What are you doing to me?" she whispered as she rested her hand on his forearm.

Burning to touch her, he placed his hand on her hip

and tugged her forward. "I could ask you the same thing," he murmured, close enough that their breaths mingled.

When their mouths met, Noah felt the power of their kiss deep in his gut. With a groan, he licked the seam of her lips and she opened to him, their tongues tangling in a slow and steady mating. She whimpered into his mouth and her hands found their way around his neck as she arched forward, the tips of her toes digging into the dirt. His hand skated from her hip to her ass and he squeezed, relishing the feel of her soft flesh against his palm.

As their kiss grew hungrier and more frenzied, Noah forgot where they were. His only thought was "mine" as he backed her up against a tree. Rolling his hips so she'd feel how badly he wanted her, he trailed his mouth down her jaw to her neck. Angelica panted, and her leg came up to wrap around him. Cradled against her, he pressed his erection into the vee of her thighs with a slow thrust.

"Oh god," she moaned, her head falling back and her eyes dropping closed. "You feel so damn good."

Before Noah could tell her that she felt like nothing he'd ever experienced, Molly interrupted them with a high-pitched squeal and then a series of deep, shuddering barks. When his dog tore past hot on the tail of a rabbit, he snapped back to reality.

He captured Angelica's lips in a hard, searing kiss and then pushed away. Quickly scanning the area for his dog, he spotted her galloping up the hillside.

Noah took one last look at the woman his brain screamed belonged to him. "This isn't over. Not by a long shot."

And then he took off at a sprint.

***

"Goddamn stupid dog," Noah muttered with a shake of his head as they pulled onto the highway toward Tomales Bay. He loved Molly like nothing else in this world, but sometimes he wondered if his faithful canine companion legitimately had shit for brains.

You're the genius who let her off her leash, so what does that say about you? his subconscious queried. Okay, so maybe he'd stupidly given Molly too much off-leash time lately, but when she looked up at him with those big sad eyes of hers, just begging to be allowed to roam free, who was he to deny her? Still, lesson learned. His dog was not to be trusted.

"You look like you want to murder something. Or more specifically, poor Molly back there." Angelica chuckled and jerked her thumb over her shoulder to indicate the recalcitrant pooch lying flat on her stomach in the back of the truck, her head resting glumly between her front paws.

Noah relaxed his face, not realizing that he'd been scowling.

"That's better," Angelica remarked, as they passed

over a rise and the glittering bay below came into view. "Oooh, that's pretty."

"It is," Noah agreed. He'd traveled all over the globe, visiting some amazing places, but this part of California—with its rolling, vine-dotted hillsides, towering trees that reached hundreds of feet into the sky, and crystalline, nutrient-rich waters—was his favorite.

Pulling the truck to the side of the road, he threw it in park and turned the ignition. "We're here."

He let Molly out the back and took her leash in one hand and Angelica's hand in the other. Crossing the road, Noah led them to a bluff overlooking a quiet, empty inlet. Dropping her hand, he pointed off to the distance. "See that shack down there?"

Angelica shielded her eyes from the high mid-afternoon sun and squinted. "The white one?"

Noah grinned. "Yup. That's where we're heading."

Angelica's eyes flashed with concern, and then she glanced down to her feet. "Are you sure?" She was wearing a pair of Converse that normally he wouldn't recommend for hiking, but the trail down wasn't too treacherous. Besides, he was there to help her.

"Absolutely," he said, grabbing her hand again and tugging her forward. As they began their slow descent toward the water line, he explained, "It's a little tricky the first part of the way, but after we get past that tree —" he jutted his chin in the direction of a lone oak "—it flattens out into a pretty meadow and then it's a nice stroll along the water for a few hundred feet."

When they reached another steep descent, Noah turned to watch Angelica's climb down. She was chewing her lip and scrunching up her nose as she focused on putting one foot carefully in front of the other so as not to slip and fall. It was cute and endearing, and it reminded him that she was a city girl at heart.

Noah wrapped Molly's leash around a small sapling and nudged the dog into laying down. When Molly's nose met her paws in a sleepy droop,Noah gripped Angelica's waist and hoisted her the remaining few feet. "I got you." But instead of setting her down, he held her tight against him, her feet dangling above the ground.

Her eyes locked on his and she smiled down at him. "Well, hello. We meet again."

"I can't seem to keep my hands off you." He lowered her a bit and then took her lips in a slow, savoring kiss. "Or my mouth."

"Remind me why we're here again." Her tongue darted out to caress her bottom lip.

"I'm supposed to be feeding you. Remember?"

He loosened his hold, and Angelica slid down the length of his body until her feet were firmly planted on the grass.

"What if I'm hungry for something else?" she asked, her voice bold, as her fingers danced to the waistband of his cargo shorts.

Noah sucked in a breath and held it, his heart thumping heavily in his chest as he waited to see what she would do next. When her fingers dipped between the fabric and his skin and then ventured south, Noah's breath left him entirely.

"Angelica."

"Shh," she murmured, eliminating the distance between them. "Let me touch you. I've been dying to get my hands on you all day."

With gritted teeth Noah nodded, giving her permission to explore. When she palmed his cock and squeezed, he saw stars. It took everything in his power not to thrust his hips forward and demand more.

"I want you so bad right now," she said, rubbing up against him like a cat.

Reaching down to still her roving hand, Noah captured Angelica's lips in a quick kiss before asking, "Do you trust me?"

She studied him, no hesitation whatsoever in her eyes, and nodded. "Absolutely."

"And you know I didn't plan this?"

Angelica giggled, and the tinkling sound of her laughter had Noah's balls drawing tight. God, what she did to him.

"I'm pretty sure you couldn't have planned for me to get handsy with your dick in the middle of a field."

Noah's lips hitched up. "No, I couldn't have planned for that," he agreed. "But you won't ever hear me complain about your hands stroking my cock."

Angelica shivered, her pupils dilated, and Noah knew she was right there with him.

Turning to Molly, he told her to lay down and stay. For once, she thankfully complied. Then he led

Angelica down the path until they reached the grassy clearing beyond the oak he'd pointed out before.

Without preamble, he pulled her into his arms, fisted her ponytail, and captured her lips in a fiery kiss meant to dominate and devour. He licked his way inside her mouth, desperate to have a part of him-any part-inside of her.

"Noah," Angelica moaned when he pulled his lips away to lick a wet, hot path down her neck. "Yes," she squeaked when his mouth moved south to suck her breast through her tank top, leaving a wet mark around her nipple.

He cupped her through her shorts and pressed with his palm. She groaned, and her hips jutted forward.

"Are you with me?" he asked, the question sounding more like a demanding growl than he'd intended.

Her eyes whipped around, taking in their location, and he could see the hesitancy written on her face.

"Don't worry, there's no one here. We're miles from anyone.

"Are you sure?"

He kissed her, slow and sweet this time. "Yes, I own this land. Or, my family does. The only other person who ever uses it is a family friend and he's not here."

"How do you know?"

He chuckled. "Because I called him at dawn and told him to get lost."

Angelica's eyes went wide, and she tried to stifle a laugh, but failed. "I thought you said you didn't plan this."

Despite her twinkling eyes, Noah could hear the doubt creeping into her voice.

He skated his fingertips along the slope of her shoulder and down her arm, until he reached her hand. Threading their fingers together, he said, "I planned on bringing you out here for lunch. That's all. We've got two bags of oysters waiting for us, and the grill is ready to light. I was going to feed you, and then I was going to take you home, praying the entire drive back that you feel even half of what I feel for you."

He swallowed deep. He hadn't meant to reveal so much so soon, but if he wanted this woman in his bed, he knew he needed to be real with her. They'd talked about a friends-with-benefits arrangement, but his heart was telling him there was more to their connection than that.

"From the moment I laid eyes on you, I wanted you," he continued. "You take my breath away." He took Angelica's other hand and wrapped them both around his neck. When he dropped his arms, hers remained locked tight around him. "And right now, I want-more than anything in the world-to make you feel the same."

Angelica licked her lips and her gaze grew cloudy with desire. "You already do."

"Not like this, I haven't," Noah promised as he lowered them to their knees. And then he kissed her until he was completely and utterly lost in the taste and feel of her, this maddening, exasperating, sexy, wonderful, delightful woman that he never saw coming.

Easing Angelica onto her back, the tall blades of swaying grass wrapping them in a feathery cocoon, Noah took his time removing her clothes, unwrapping her like the precious gift that she was. And then they took turns exploring one another-his hands learning every curve and valley of her body, while she mapped out every sharp dip and plane of his.

"I need you," Angelica breathed, reaching for him after he'd coaxed a climax from her with fingers, lips, and tongue. "Please, Noah."

He kissed the inside of her thigh and sat back on his haunches. Reaching into his wallet, he pulled out a condom and rolled it over his cock.

Angelica bit her lip and slid her thighs wider, giving him enough room to settle between them.

"Say it again," he demanded.

The words themselves weren't what mattered. They were simple things, uttered all the damn time in the heat of passion. But when Angelica said them, they called to something wild and primitive deep inside of him. When she begged, he lost all sense of himself. Her pleasure was the only thing that mattered -- and that he was the one delivering it.

"I need you," she repeated. "Please Noah, fuck me."

With that entreaty, he thrust forward, burying himself deep inside of her.

Angelica's back arched off the ground and she wrapped her legs around his waist. "Oh my god! Oh shit. Oh god!"

With each driving thrust, Noah thought she had the

right of it. Because if this wasn't heaven, he didn't know what was.

And when they came together, her nails raking down his back and his name on her lips, Noah thought he could die a happy man.

CHAPTER TEN

The oysters were good, but they were nothing compared to the sex. Angelica licked her fingers lazily, enjoying the warm juices from the grilled oyster she'd just tipped into her mouth almost as much as she enjoyed the way Noah's eyes were following her every move. A repeat of their earlier activities seemed inevitable, and she wasn't complaining. It had been the best sex she'd had in years. Maybe ever. In the middle of a meadow. Who knew?

"That was the last one," Noah said, his eyes not leaving her lips.

"Sorry," she said. "Did you want it?"

"I want something," he said.

"Mmm. Such as?"

He smiled lazily. "You. Again."

Her hands rose to the collar of her shirt almost without realizing it. She suspected his hot stare could get her naked without him saying a word.

"Wait," he said, breaking into her thoughts.

"What?" Her hands froze.

"Let's go back to my place." When she hesitated, he must have thought the worst, because he hurried on. "I just meant there's a bed. A big one? And, uh, a shower. You said that the plumbing—"

"Yes."

"Yes?"

"Yes, let's go back to your place. You had me at shower." She grinned at him. "I mean, sex too, but you really sold me with the shower."

His warm chuckle followed her as she swept discarded oyster shells and their lunch plates and napkins into a bag as quickly as possible. "You're easily bribed, Angelica."

"You live without plumbing for a weekend and see how cheap you go," she shot back.

With Molly following them, her tail sweeping a zig-zag through the waving grass, they made their way back to the truck. Once there, he backed her up against the passenger door and kissed her so thoroughly she was ready to climb him then and there.

"Noah," she gasped.

He pulled back, breathing hard and shaking his head. "No, let's go. I hate to admit it, but I might be getting too old for hot and heavy up against the seat of the truck."

When he put a hand on his back and winced dramatically, she gulped back a laugh. "Let's go, then," she said, reaching to open the door, but finding his hand already on the handle. "Oh. Thanks."

She put one foot on the truck's running board, then gasped as his hand cupped her ass with a squeeze that veered in intimate directions. Her body tilted invitingly as she leaned into the caress, and she heard him gulp behind her. Then she was unceremoniously boosted into the truck with a firm push, and the door slammed shut behind her.

"You started it," she reminded him as he practically leapt into his own seat. "Don't try to dish it out if you can't take it, Blackstone."

"Oh, we'll be dishing, all right." The truck came to life with a rumble, and his hand came to rest between her thighs as she finished buckling her seat belt.

The ride back to his house was excruciating, exhilarating, and over both far too soon and not nearly soon enough. His fingers worked their magic between her legs, slipping down beneath her pants to touch skin—and more—until she was gasping and sobbing in the seat, writhing in thwarted ecstasy.

Noah pulled the truck to a stop and they tumbled out together. Molly followed them into the house, and somehow, he remembered to free the dog from her leash before he and Angelica fell into his bedroom, shutting the door firmly in front of his dog's curious snout.

Two hours later, Angelica traced lazy circles around the outlines of muscles on Noah's chest. He yawned and trapped her hand underneath his, pressing down to flatten her palm against his body.

"I like your room," she said.

"Hmm?"

"It's very you."

"Messy?" Their clothes strewn in a path to the bed weren't the only things tossed around the room.

She chuckled, feeling her body bounce gently against his. "No, it's just …" she waved a hand. "Clean lines, good bones, interesting treasures, rustic overlay."

"That sounds like you're describing a mess."

"Rustic doesn't always mean messy."

"But it does right now."

"It's a good mess." She freed her hand and sat up. "Speaking of messes, you promised me a shower."

"I did? I think I like you dirty." He tried to pull her back down.

She could practically feel her hair squeaking. Between a hike, the salty breeze coming off the bay where they'd eaten lunch, incredibly hot sex—twice!—and the lack of a shower this morning, she was filthy. "Please."

"Can I impose conditions?"

"You can shower with me."

"Can I impose more conditions?"

"Like what?"

"Dinner?"

"Um," she breathed out, pretending to think as she rolled out of bed. "How about you shower with me, and if you're really nice, you can have dinner with me, too."

He grinned lazily. "How nice?"

She smirked back. "What's for dinner?"

He tugged her back down for a kiss, then gave her a little push toward the bathroom. "Frankie's?" he suggested.

"You did lunch, so I'm buying."

"But—"

She turned back around and poked him in the chest. "Don't argue with me."

She suspected her impulse to insist on paying might warrant some self-analysis later. Then again, the fact that she was sleeping with a man she'd sworn not to might require some serious thought, too. Not to mention a few vivid fantasies. Not that they'd ever compare to the real thing, she thought, as Noah flung mussed sheets aside to follow her to the shower.

He made her scream twice with his fingers before lifting her against the tiled wall, water streaming over both of them as their bodies rocked together, hard and fast. As she shuddered around him, she felt the entire world go dim for a moment.

Noah Blackstone was a hell of a drug.

She entered Frankie's behind Noah with a hint of something that felt suspiciously like nervousness. This restaurant was practically his home away from home. Was she intruding, she wondered as he greeted Max and the ever-present Sean. Then she straightened her shoulders and pushed those thoughts away. *The hell with that.* River Hill was her home, too. She owned the inn, and she intended to stay here. No matter what came of this … whatever it was she and Noah were doing. She had as much right to be here as he did.

Still, it wasn't hard to see the looks of surprise on Noah's friends' faces when he stepped aside to reveal her smaller form, nor did she miss the smirks they exchanged when he escorted her to a table instead of joining them at the bar.

"Looks like he's got the tacos again." Noah's voice was rich with anticipation. "I know what I'm getting." A platter of said tacos passed them on its way to an eager recipient, and Angelica laughed as Noah's entire body leaned towards it without conscious thought.

"You look like one of those cartoon dogs who float away on a smell," she teased.

"If I ever learn to levitate, it will definitely be because of food."

"Let me know when that happens." She picked up her menu and scanned it quickly. She'd been living in River Hill long enough to have grown familiar with it, but she hadn't worked her way through the entire menu yet. Frankie's wasn't the only restaurant in town, just the best one. "Ooh, falafel."

"They're good, too."

"Have you eaten everything here?"

"Of course not." She raised an eyebrow at him, and

he spread his hands defensively. "He changes the menu seasonally! I couldn't have."

She snorted, and he leaned across the table. "I can think of a few other things I'd like to—"

"What a charming couple," a familiar voice interrupted. "Are we celebrating anything special tonight?" Angelica glanced up from Noah's enticing stare to find Max grinning down at them, holding a notepad ostentatiously.

"You're not our waitress," Noah said dryly.

"I am now. What'll you have?"

Noah rolled his eyes, and Angelica smiled. She could have told him they weren't going to get through their meal without some heckling from his friends. Hopefully it would be mild. She wasn't remotely in the mood for laughter and guffaws at her expense.

Thankfully, Max ceased his ribbing and they ordered without further comment. When he left, she returned her attention to Noah, who was watching her again, his expression speculative. "What?"

"When is your plumbing going to be fixed?"

"Tomorrow morning."

His eyebrow went up. "You got the plumber to agree to come out on a Sunday?"

"I didn't give him much choice," she admitted. "Not my finest hour, but it's his fault the water's not running. It was supposed to be back up yesterday." She was actually a little proud of herself for standing her ground on the matter. The plumber's screw-ups didn't need to impact *her* schedule, and she'd told him so. Loudly.

"Well, you can shower at my place anytime."

"Thanks. If he fails to show up, you'll be hearing from me." She tossed him a grin, ignoring the tightness in her belly that tempted her to say she'd be over first thing in the morning.

Step back, girl. This was casual, she reminded herself. Incredible, mind-blowing, orgasm record-setting, but definitely casual. No matter how much she enjoyed talking to him, and watching the expressions on his face, she wasn't going to mistake it for anything else.

This wasn't L.A., where you could disappear into the city without anyone seeing your walk of shame. She wanted to stay in River Hill, become a part of the town. Here, everyone knew everyone else, and her business might depend on good relationships with other businesses. Like Noah's, and Max's, and others who were watching the happenings in their little booth with interest.

Time to change the subject. "Are you still working on adjusting the vines on the driveway?"

He gave her a glance she couldn't interpret, but he didn't push anymore about his shower offer. "Yeah. It looks like they've rooted really well. We won't see any grapes until next year, so we'll take the time this fall to give them a really solid structure to grow on, and adjust the soil if we need to."

She nodded like she had some idea of what he was talking about. "Makes sense."

"What about you?"

"What about me?"

"The plumber is fixing the upstairs bathrooms, right?"

"Yeah, we switched out the fixtures in two of them, and just fixed the leak in the master."

"You didn't replace anything in the master?"

"I couldn't give up the clawfoot tub," she said with a blissful sigh. "It's incredible."

"Is there a shower?"

"You seem awfully interested in my shower situation," she joked.

He smiled, a dimple peeking through the rough hair on his jaw. "Can you blame me?"

"There's a shower," she said. "Separate standing one. That's what was leaking, actually. Apparently, it took longer to find the faulty pipe than he expected, and he had to leave his fix to cure before he could turn the water back on."

"I know literally nothing about plumbing, so I'll have to take your word for it," Noah said.

"I don't know much either," she answered, "but I made him explain everything he was doing." If she was going to renovate, she was going to do it right, which meant learning about all the things that could possibly go wrong in her new-old house.

"On camera?"

She made a face. "Apparently plumbing isn't glamorous enough to bother filming. They did a few shots in the morning for the easy fixes, but they left us to do the hard stuff alone."

"Your tacos, worthy gentleman," said a new voice.

"You are *definitely* not our waitress," Noah said to Sean, who was gleefully placing their plates in front of them.

Angelica glanced to the side and saw Max grinning at them while the waitress who usually served this section was rolling her eyes and pocketing what looked like a twenty-dollar bill.

"Did you bribe Jenny?" she asked.

"Do I look like somebody who would bribe a waitress?"

"Yes," she and Noah answered in unison.

"I'm offended."

"I'm offended that Max let you do it." Noah spun his plate to angle his tacos in the right direction to line up with his mouth.

"It was his idea."

"Of course it was."

Angelica took a bite of her dinner and let the two of them banter for a minute or two before she interrupted. "Did you want to get your joke out of the way before the tacos get cold?" She smiled sweetly up at Sean, who looked startled, then pretended to be wounded.

"Can't a guy bring his best friend tacos once in awhile?"

"Sure, if that guy learns that waiters usually leave after they've delivered the food," Noah grumbled.

"Good ones ask how you're doing," Sean said.

"We're fine. Go away."

"Sure you don't need anything? Candlelight? Rose petals?"

Angelica snickered as Noah aimed a fork at Sean's wrist. "Go!"

"Fine! Geez, the customer isn't always right, you know." Sean dodged the fork and gave Angelica a wave as he scurried back to the bar.

"That was much better than I expected," she said.

"You expected it?"

"You didn't?" She looked at him, genuinely surprised. "You show up at your favorite restaurant with me in tow, and come to a table instead of the bar with your friends, and you don't expect them to say anything?"

His eyebrows drew down, and he looked chagrined. "When you put it that way…"

She shrugged. "They were perfectly nice about it."

"I suppose. Sean should probably stick to his day job, though."

"Waiting tables probably isn't his calling," she agreed with a laugh.

"I thought he was going to drop your plate in your lap."

"Half of your tacos are out of their shell," she pointed out. "Balance apparently isn't his strong suit."

He laughed and used his fork to scoop the filling back into his tortilla. "Max will never let him do it again, even for a prank. His plating is too important."

"Max's food is amazing," she said. He nodded agreement, mouth already full.

After a few more bites, she sat back and took a deep breath. "So, are we going to talk about this?"

He swallowed. "The food?"

"Not the food." She shook her head slowly.

"Oh."

"Yeah."

Noah eyed her, and she felt a riot of conflicting emotions ripple through her body.

"You first," he said finally.

She rolled her eyes. "Fine. It's still Friendship Day, right?"

Casual. Keep it casual.

"Yesss." He drew the word out slowly, still watching her. "So we're friends?"

"With benefits?" she suggested hopefully.

"Oh, thank God." He sounded truly heartfelt, and she couldn't help laughing.

"I'm not an idiot, Noah. Nobody gives up sex that good."

"I agree. Wholeheartedly."

She smiled down into her plate. "I had a great day." She looked up and met his eyes. "Thank you. For all of it, not just … you know."

He smiled back, and she basked in the warmth of his gaze. "I did, too. All of it."

"So, should we have another Friendship Day soon?"

"As soon as possible," he agreed around a mouthful

of taco. "I'll come over and break some more of your plumbing, if it'll help facilitate things."

"Gee, thanks."

"I'm a really good friend," he said with a grin.

That was certainly the truth.

Angelica couldn't *wait* for the next Friendship Day.

CHAPTER ELEVEN

Noah stretched, his calf muscles pulling taut as he arched his foot with a groan. Even though he worked out regularly and was in relatively good shape for a thirty-five-year-old, yesterday he'd exerted his body in ways he hadn't in a good long while and this morning he was feeling it. He rolled to his side and grabbed his phone off the nightstand to check the time and then set it back down.

Nine o'clock. How was that even possible? He hadn't slept that late in ages.

You haven't fucked that long and that well in ages either, his subconscious reminded him.

That was certainly true. He'd known he and Angelica had amazing chemistry, but never in his wildest dreams had he thought they would be quite so explosive together. Even all these hours later, he swore he could still feel her lips on his skin. With that thought in mind, he took his morning wood in hand, intent on reliving all the ways they'd pleasured one another when he was startled out of his reverie by the ringing of his phone.

He ignored it, hoping whoever was calling would take a hint and hang up. When the ringing finally stopped, he screwed his eyes shut and tried to recapture the feeling of Angelica's soft curves beneath him. When it started ringing again, the chorus from Michael Jackson's "Leave Me Alone" echoed through his bedroom.

"Ah, for fuck's sake." His eyes popped open and he let go of his dick. Picking up the phone and bringing it to his ear, he said, "This better be good, mother."

"Well hello to you too, dear," she responded. "Why haven't you sent in your RSVP for the charity gala next weekend?"

"I'm busy that night."

"Doing what?"

"Watching paint dry."

"Noah Carter Bradstone. Don't you get smart with me."

He groaned. "Sorry, mother."

"Apology accepted. Now, who are you bringing?"

His first instinct was to tell her he'd met someone, but then he recalled his and Angelica's conversation at the restaurant. They were friends with benefits, nothing more. And while the benefits were quite exceptional, the friends part was what was important here. They might have spent an awesome day together, but the gala was on a whole other level. He would be photographed extensively with whoever he brought as his date, and that's not what he and Angelica were about. Even though her time in Hollywood had probably desensitized her to the pomp and circumstance of a black-tie event, he couldn't really picture her mingling with the doyens of the San Francisco elite. Hell, he could barely picture doing it himself and he'd been born into their rarified ranks. If he was being honest, he enjoyed the fact that Angelica didn't know *that* Noah, didn't expect him to be that buffed and polished version of himself.

But if he didn't take Angelica, where did that leave him? Before he could open his mouth, his mother had the answer. "You know, Naomi Klein is such a lovely girl, and you make the most adorable couple."

He pinched the bridge of his nose. "First of all, Naomi is not a *girl*; she's a woman. A very successful one at that, and I know for a fact she'd hate it if she knew you talked about her like she was some naïve debutante."

"You know what I mean, dear." He could practically picture her brushing his comment aside with a wave of her hand.

And even though Noah knew his mother would probably ignore his next comment too, he soldiered on. "And second of all, we are not a couple. I've told you that a hundred times. Naomi and I are friends. That's it."

"That's not what I hear," she replied coyly. "Soraya Morrow saw Naomi leaving your tasting room well after dark last month." With a tinkling laugh, she added, "And you and I both know what happens between a man and a woman once they get a few glasses of wine in them."

Noah held back a shudder. He'd heard this story often enough he could practically recite it himself, and he still wished he'd never been told. No son needed to know he'd been conceived on his father's tasting room bar after his parents had cracked open a bottle of the latest vintage of Bradstone Family Vineyards Cabernet Sauvignon.

"That was a business meeting."

"Hmm. Is that what they're calling it nowadays?"

"She's designing my new wine labels," he countered.

"Of course she is, dear."

Noah sighed in defeat. There was no getting through to his mother when she got like this. Pit bulls had nothing on Bernice Louise Winchester Bradstone.

"All right, mother. I'll ask Naomi if she's free. I'm not making any guarantees though. She might be busy that night."

She laughed. "Oh Noah, you're a hoot sometimes. You know the Kleins would never let their only daughter skip out on the most important gala of the year. Especially not when her mother practically runs the committee and her father is gunning for the Chief of Staff position at the hospital next year."

Shit. She had a point.

The last time Dr. Klein had pushed to move up in the ranks at San Francisco's largest hospital, he'd dragged his beautiful and intelligent daughter to every event he attended in the hopes that she'd boost his public persona. The hospital's Board of Directors loved Naomi. She was a credit to the Klein name and everyone in that family knew it.

For the next year, he suspected Naomi would be forced into attending three times the number of events as usual, no matter how much she hated it. Her father was a perfectly good surgeon. Couldn't he score the hospital directorship on his own? Apparently not.

But he didn't want to give his mom the satisfaction of admitting that she might be right. He and Naomi had both managed to carve out lives for themselves outside of the glitz and glamour of their vaunted family names. But secretly, they'd admitted to one another that when their parents really wanted something from either of them, they mostly acquiesced. Noah had often thought things would be so much easier if neither he nor Naomi actually liked their parents. Disappointing them would have been less tortuous than being trotted out for the dog and pony show they'd been enduring their whole lives.

"I'll call Naomi later today to find out if she's going. If she is, and she doesn't already have a date, we'll do the media line together."

"And dance together," his mother bargained.

"Maybe."

"It's just one dance, Noah. I don't know why you have to be so recalcitrant. You like Naomi, don't you?"

"Yes, mom. You know full well she's one of my closest friends."

"I always did say the best love affairs were built on solid friendships."

"Bye, mother."

"Goodbye, Noah. See you for lunch on Wednesday."

Once he'd showered, Noah puttered around the house catching up on email and then watching an episode of his favorite show on Netflix. And through it all, he wondered what Angelica was up to. Had she woken up thinking about him? Were her muscles sore from exertion, too? He was about to pick up his phone to call her when there was a knock at his door.

"Yoo hoo," Naomi called as she pushed through the screen with a box in her hands. "I've got your labels." She set them down on the entry hall table.

"You didn't have to bring them here, especially on the weekend. I could have picked them up from you later."

"It's okay," she said, swiping her palms down her paint-spattered jeans to clean them off. "I wanted to come by anyhow so we could talk." Naomi was tall and slender, with her father's dark, wavy hair and her mother's high, pale forehead. She spent most of her time in her studio, so her skin stayed practically translucent. Noah was pretty sure his friend hadn't seen the actual outdoors in years other than from inside the tinted windows of her Mercedes.

"Talk?" Noah asked, worried where this might be going.

He hadn't lied to his mother. Naomi *was* one of his closest friends, but they'd blurred the lines of that friendship pretty frequently over the years, and he'd never quite gotten comfortable with where that might eventually leave them. They'd promised not to fall in love with one another, and while he really didn't think that would be a problem, he couldn't help but flinch any time a woman said they needed to talk. More often than not, the relationship discussion followed.

"It appears you're taking me to the gala next weekend."

He groaned. "Yeah, my mom called this morning and roped me into going. I tried to get out of it, but you know how she is."

"Better than most." She dropped into the distressed leather chair across from him and took a swig of his beer.

"Hey, get your own."

"I will," she said with an impish grin. "After I've finished yours."

"Bitch."

"Asshole."

They smiled at each other, the familiar insults ones they'd been trading for more than two decades.

"So, what time are you picking me up?" she asked,

tipping back the bottle. True to her word, she'd emptied the last dregs of his favorite IPA.

"Does eight o'clock work for you?"

Her lips pursed, and she looked to the ceiling. "Seven would probably be better."

"But that means we'll get there early."

"It means we can leave early, too."

"Good point," he acknowledged, pushing off the sofa to grab another bottle. "You want one?" he asked over his shoulder as he stepped into the kitchen.

"No thanks, I have to drive down to Sausalito tonight for a gallery opening."

Noah groaned. If there was anything he hated more than going to galas it was schmoozing at hoity-toity galleries. That was one of the reasons he and Naomi would never have worked as a couple. As an in-demand sculptor, she spent most of her free nights in them—by choice—while he'd find any excuse to avoid them.

When he came back into the room, she was staring at him with a look on her face he couldn't interpret. And that had him worried. After twenty years, he thought he knew all her expressions.

"What?" he asked, settling into the soft cushions of his worn leather sofa. "You're staring. You know I hate it when you stare."

"You don't have to be my date, you know."

He shrugged. "I know. But it's kind of our thing by now."

"You could take someone else if you wanted."

He chuckled and shook his head. "And who would I possibly take? You know for a fact every woman I've ever brought to one of these things thought it meant a ring was forthcoming. No thanks." He raised the bottle to hips lips and drank down a few deep gulps.

"You could take Angelica Travis."

Noah choked on his beer and his eyes watered as he fought back his coughing fit. He hadn't told Naomi about Angelica yet, but he *had* been wondering how to bring it up without coming off like an asshole.

It'd been months since they'd last fooled around, but Noah was smart enough not to talk about the new woman he was fucking with the one he'd once fucked on the regular—no matter how close of a friend she might be. While their particular situation had never been covered in one of the umpteen etiquette courses his mother had forced him to attend, he knew doing so would be poor form any way you sliced it.

"Angelica?" he asked, going for nonchalant and failing.

"Oh, come off it. Her camera crew is a big bunch of gossips, and they hit the bar almost every night."

"Those fuckers. I knew I didn't like them."

She laughed. "And I just came from Frankie's. Max confirmed everything."

"What did that rat bastard confirm?"

Naomi tilted her head and studied him, like she might one of her sculptures as she searched out any obvious flaw in her work. "You're into her," she eventually said.

"She's my neighbor, and we're friends."

She raised one of her perfectly groomed eyebrows. "Like you and I have been friends?"

Noah didn't often blush, but when he did, he did so all the way to roots of his hair and to the tips of his ears. He felt like he was twelve years old again, seeing his first pair of breasts. When his face was so hot it felt like it was going to melt off, he broke her stare and looked away. "It's not like that."

"No, I suppose not," she sighed.

Uh oh, what does that tone mean? he asked himself as he brought his face back around to study his lifelong friend. *She's not disappointed, is she?*

"You're not … I mean … you didn't think …" He couldn't even bring himself to ask the question.

Naomi took his meaning immediately and laughed uproariously. "Oh god, no. You and me? No, absolutely not." She wiped a tear from her eye. "That'd be an unmitigated disaster. You're hot, Noah, and I love you, but I don't love you like *that*."

"Then what was all that about?" He waved in her general direction.

"You're getting old."

"Speak for yourself. I'm in the prime of my life."

She shot him fake daggers. "And I don't look a day over twenty-five."

Now it was his turn to study Naomi. By any objective measure, she was a beautiful woman. Months ago, he would have freely admitted she was the *most* beautiful woman he'd ever been with, but since meeting

Angelica, no one else compared. But his friend was right. She didn't look her age. And yet he couldn't let her get the final word in. "Not a day over thirty, at least."

"Fuck you!" she laughed, and he smirked in response. "You're just being an asshole because you loooove her." She dragged the word out like a fifth grader, her hands clenched in front of her chest and her eyebrows batting exaggeratingly.

Their easy ribbing was one of the things he valued most about their friendship. Noah knew she'd never take offense to anything he said, and vice versa. On the flip side, he and Angelica had been sniping at one another since practically the first moment they'd met. While it wasn't conventional flirting, it certainly kept his blood hot. One thing was for certain, Angelica made him feel alive.

He took another swig of his beer. "I do *not* love her. I love her ass, and yes, I *like* her, but you're getting way ahead of yourself."

"Rumor has it you and Angelica look good together. Like really good."

"What's that even mean?"

"It means she's Marilyn Monroe and you're—" she peered at him assessingly. "Well, I don't know who you are, but whoever it is, he's one handsome devil."

"Oh yeah?" Noah knew he was an attractive man, but Angelica was fucking stunning. If people thought they looked good together, it was only because they'd been blinded by her incandescent beauty.

"Yeah," Naomi confirmed. "And I also heard you couldn't stop smiling." She pointed at his face. "Like that."

He forced his lips to relax. "I wasn't smiling."

"You were *so* smiling."

"All right," he admitted. "I was smiling."

He needed to caution his friend not to go getting any ideas about him and Angelica though. "It's not serious. Neither of us is looking for anything permanent."

"Are you sure?"

Noah paused. *Was* he sure? If Naomi had asked him the same question a couple of days ago, he wouldn't have hesitated to answer. He absolutely was *not* looking for a relationship. And yet, his Friendship Day with Angelica had been perfect. *She'd* been perfect. If being with her meant days like that—followed by *nights* like that—he might reconsider his position.

But he was a practical man, too.

As much as he craved his sexy neighbor's company now, he didn't believe those feelings would last. In time, they'd discover each other's faults, pick at them, and wind up fighting all the damn time. Which was reason enough not to go down that road. He truly liked Angelica; he couldn't imagine one day hating her too.

"Yeah, I'm sure."

Now if only he actually believed that.

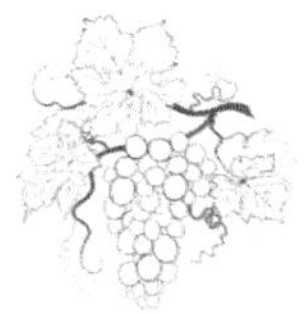

CHAPTER TWELVE

*L*eaning closer to hear the naughty suggestions Noah was making through the steam of their coffees, Angelica almost didn't hear her name being called.

"Miss Travis! Miss Travis!" An older man, almost impossibly skinny, was pushing through the crowd of people that inevitably thronged River Hill's favorite coffee shop.

The Hollow Bean had incredible coffee—the best Angelica had ever tasted—but the little storefront on Main Street had an absolutely terrible layout. It was something to do with the historic nature of the building, she'd heard. Apparently, they couldn't change it, so they had to figure out how to work with it. And so all the coffee-drinkers of River Hill had learned very quickly how to do a very specific dance-and-shuffle to get their fix. In general, everything moved smoothly. Unless somebody disrupted the flow, like now.

"Mayor Rideout?" Angelica shifted aside to make room for the man, letting the crowd reform around him like Jell-o. "Can I help you?"

"I hope so," the mayor said with a genial smile. "Hello, Mr. Blackstone."

"Hi," said Noah, eyeing the man. He didn't appear happy at having their quick coffee date interrupted. They both had busy days, so running into each other this morning had been a lucky break.

"What can I do for you?" Angelica asked. She wasn't particularly thrilled about the interruption either, but she was at least capable of putting on a polite face. Grumpy Noah was on full display.

"Do you have time for a meeting later today? The Council and I have a proposition we'd like to discuss with you."

She raised her eyebrows in surprise, and then glanced at Noah, who shrugged, apparently just as baffled as she was. "Let me check my schedule," she said, pulling her phone out of her pocket and opening up her calendar. "Would four o'clock work? I think I'm done filming at three, and I'm not meeting with the countertop measurers until six."

"That would be perfect." The mayor awarded her a sunny smile, stretching his face into a complicated series of curves and wrinkles under his shock of fluffy gray hair. "Thank you. We can come to you, if that's easiest?"

"Uh, sure." She didn't exactly have a conference

room, but the dining room was at least mostly finished. "Sounds good."

"Wonderful! We'll see you then." The mayor shook her hand, gave Noah a nod, and then destroyed several more people's Monday mornings by again disrupting the flow of traffic in the tiny shop as he made his way to the door.

"What was that about?" Angelica turned to Noah.

He shrugged again. "I have no idea. Maybe they want you to donate something for the Harvest Festival, since you're the newest small business in town."

"Is that a thing?"

He nodded. "I usually send a couple cases of wine. Sometimes they use it for prizes, sometimes they serve it during the pre-festival dinner."

"Let me guess. Max donates his time for the dinner?"

"And most of the farms donate the food, yeah."

"It's dinner for the entire town?"

"Pretty much. They do up the square over there for the festival." He tilted his chin toward the window that looked out on River Hill's town square, an ornate Victorian gazebo at its center. "And the whole town participates, so the Council hosts a huge thank-you dinner for the volunteers before the festival opens. Banquet tables on the square, a big buffet, you know."

"Sounds fun," she said. "I love festivals."

"Please tell me you're not the sort of person who buys every handmade straw basket in sight."

"I mean, who can resist a really well-made basket?" she teased.

"God help us all." He rested his forehead on his palm in mock despair, and she laughed.

"Don't even start. I saw that inlaid wood clock on your wall. And the watercolors."

He raised a finger. "But I guarantee you did not see any baskets."

She shook her head. "Not yet."

"You're a menace," he said with a smile. "I've gotta go. See you later?"

She nodded, and they followed the line back out the door with the ease of practiced customers before they went their separate ways.

"Ugh. How am I supposed to have time to go to all of these events?" Angelica waved the sheaf of papers that had been dropped off by a courier toward Leah, who was packing up her supplies.

"You make time, honey," Leah said. "Do you need makeup remover?" She held up a large bottle of blue liquid.

"No, I've got some, but thanks." Angelica looked back down at the paper. "This schedule is insane. There are six promotional appearances, two premieres, and a charity gala. All in the next three weeks. Do they not understand that they hired me to film a renovation?"

"Angelica, you're the star of a TV show. This is what

they do. TV runs on advertising revenue, and you're the honey to lure those commercial flies." Leah snapped her makeup case closed. "Call them and ask to rework the schedule if you have conflicts, but you're still going to have to do the work."

Angelica sighed. "I know. "

"Did you find out what the mayor wants?"

"No, but he'll be here in about an hour."

"Well, I'll leave you to change, then."

"What, you don't have meetings with mayors with caulk on your shirt?" Angelica laughed.

"I try not to get into these sticky situations." Leah's voice faded as she headed out the door with a final wave.

Angelica looked down at the schedule again, and then grabbed a pen from the counter. "If I ask to take this one off the list and replace it with something later, and move this one … " She scribbled notes and crossed things off until the paper was practically unreadable. "There. That should work," she pronounced with a satisfied nod.

Having devised a schedule that was much more manageable, she fired off an email to the RenoTV promotional department staffer who was listed at the top of the sheet. Based on her upcoming construction schedule, she could handle three promotional events and a charity gala over the next two weeks. With a quick glance down her body and a purse of her lips, she realized she was going to have to improve her wardrobe, however.

Speaking of which, she glanced at the clock on the microwave. "Oops." No time for a shower, but she could at least change into clean clothes for the mayor. He probably wouldn't notice a ponytail.

Ten minutes later and freshly clothed, she opened the door to greet Mayor Rideout and two older women. "Come on in."

"Thank you. Angelica, this is Mary Amory and Patricia Lockwood."

"Nice to meet you." She waved them in and pointed to the left. "Will the dining room work? It's the most finished room I've got."

Mary Amory, a dark-haired woman with a friendly smile, nodded. "No problem."

They all trooped into the room and seated themselves around the long oak table before Angelica connected the dots. "Are you related to Sean Amory, by chance?"

Mary smiled again. "He's my son, actually."

"Oh! I know him," Angelica finished rather lamely. Hard to explain that she knew this woman's son because she was exuberantly fucking said son's good friend.

"Mary and Patricia are both small business owners who are on the town council," the mayor said.

"I see." She didn't, really, so she asked, "So what can I do for you?"

"Well, I'm sure you know that word spreads relatively quickly around here," Mary said with a grin.

Angelica fought to cool the blush she could feel start-ing. Surely they weren't talking about her and Noah?

"We know you're shooting a TV show here," Patricia said.

"And we're all very excited about it," the mayor added. "We were wondering if you might be open to expanding the scope of your filming a little bit."

Angelica blinked. "What do you mean?"

"We thought it would be lovely if on your show you could walk around town a little, being sure to mention how nice River Hill is. It could be a lovely little boost," Mayor Rideout explained.

"Tourism is a big deal here," Mary interjected, "and since you're going to be opening an inn, you'll want to be a part of the town's tourism board, I expect."

"I … guess so?"

"If you're willing, we thought that your camera crew could film some of the preparations for the Harvest Festival. Or even the festival itself, if you're still going to be filming by then. It really is our town at its best." The mayor straightened his shoulders proudly.

"Oh. Oh, I see." Angelica tried to redirect her brain, and think more about the show, its promotional value, and tourism. "That's actually a really good idea."

And she wasn't just blowing smoke up their behinds. If she was really going to become a part of this community, it behooved her to do her best to help it. And River Hill was a gorgeous town. It would defi-nitely film well.

"I'm not the person in charge of production, but I think the network producers would be willing to listen if I suggested it. Local color can only add to the show." She was already drafting the email in her head. The network executive she'd signed the contract with had made lots of references to how cute River Hill was. It was going to be an easy sell.

"Wonderful," the mayor said, beaming. "I'm so excited to have you here, Miss Travis."

"The feeling's definitely mutual, sir," she said.

As she showed the trio out, she tried to identify the warmth coursing through her. Was it a feeling of welcome? Belonging? Years spent in Hollywood didn't exactly make for a sense of community. She'd never felt so involved in anything before, so committed to a place and a group of people. It was nice, she realized with a big grin.

And the urge to talk to somebody about this realization was strong, so without thinking, she dialed Noah's cell phone.

"What's up?" He sounded like he was outdoors. Unsurprising.

"Is this a bad time?" For all she was sleeping with the man, she knew very little about how he actually spent the bulk of his days.

"Nah. Just checking on some stuff in the vines. You?"

"The mayor just left. Oh, and I met Sean's mom."

"Wow, he pulled out the big guns?"

"Sean's mom is a big gun?"

"The Amorys have owned that bakery pretty much since the town came into existence. She's like the Aristotelian ideal of a small business owner."

"And here I thought she was just a nice lady."

"Oh, she's that, too. What did they want?"

"Get this. They wanted me to film the Harvest Festival for the show. Isn't that a great idea?" There was a long silence on the other end of the line. "Noah? You still there?"

"I'm here."

"Sorry, I must have been breaking up a little. They want me to—"

"—I heard."

"Oh." *What?* Why wasn't he saying anything? "Isn't it a great idea?"

"I don't know."

"Well, it is." She didn't know why she was snapping at him, but Grumpy Noah always brought out the worst in her. "It'll be great for tourism, it'll be great color for the show, and it'll be fantastic for my personal brand."

"Thank goodness for your personal brand," he said. The phone didn't distort the annoyance in his voice.

"I'm still trying to make a living, you know," she said. She was a business owner. An entrepreneur. He, of all people, ought to understand that. And if he was her friend like he'd said, he should be supporting her too.

"I know," he answered, sounding tired.

"Maybe I should just let you go," she said with a

feeling of regret. It had obviously been a bad idea to call him. "You seem busy."

"That's fine."

"So … I'll talk to you later, I guess."

"Yeah, talk to you later." There was a click, and then her phone went silent. She lowered it and stared at its darkened screen. What on earth had *that* been about? She knew Noah wasn't into the Hollywood lifestyle, but could he really object to a boost for his beloved town's economic potential?

She shook her head. The man was a mystery. An incredibly annoying one. Thank God she was just using him for sex.

Right?

So why did she have this sharp sinking feeling in the pit of her stomach?

CHAPTER THIRTEEN

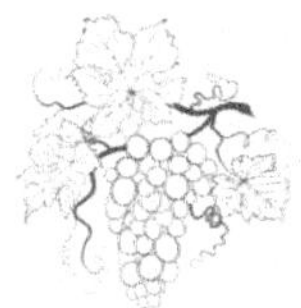

$\mathcal{N}$oah tried to tell himself he didn't care what Angelica did with her free time, or how she chose to promote her business. But the idea that she'd leverage *his* town to boost *her* "personal brand" left him feeling pricklier than usual.

And if experience had taught him anything, it was only a matter of time until she'd ask if they could film in his vineyards—or want something even larger from him. Like sponsorship or some other financial investment in the endeavor. The Bradstone name got everyone excited, and unfortunately, it seemed like Angelica wasn't the exception, after all.

He cracked open a soda and settled in at his desk to go over some important paperwork he'd been putting off. He'd gotten his MBA so he wouldn't have to outsource these tasks, but now he wondered if it wouldn't be better to hire the same firm his father used. It went against everything he wanted for

Stonewell Vineyards and himself, but as he stared at row after row on the spreadsheet he considered it might be time to put pride aside for practicality.

For the next few minutes, he shuffled papers and compared the sums on his receipts to the numbers on his screen, but his heart wasn't in it. In addition to not being able to reconcile the two totals, he couldn't stop thinking about his stilted conversation with Angelica. Lord, that woman could get under his skin like no one else.

When one of the spreadsheets he was working in crashed his computer, he blew out a frustrated breath and pushed away from his desk. Yeah, he was definitely going to have to put in a call to his dad's accountant. In the meantime, he had a few other calls to make.

"Hey man, you want to head on over to Scallywags?" Noah asked when Max picked up his phone.

"On a Monday night?"

"Ugh, good point."

The small, pirate-themed waterfront bar was normally a good place to while away a few hours in a low-key environment, but in an effort to boost revenue, last summer the owner had announced Mondays were ladies' night. While normally that wouldn't have been a problem, the women who were affiliated with the local biker gang had claimed Mondays as theirs, and they weren't shy about their appreciation for the town's younger men. One word from Big Mitch about keeping their hands off his women, and Mondays at The Scallywag were forever off the agenda.

"Sean said something about heading to The Hut tonight," Max offered.

That news gave him pause. Sean had moved back to River Hill after a pop star he'd represented had died from a heroin overdose. He'd felt responsible for the kid's death, and needing a change of scenery, had quit his label and moved home to figure out what came next in his life. He'd been working at the family bakery ever since, and Noah and Max had thought he was finally moving forward. Except, if he was drinking alone on a Monday night at the local dive bar, maybe Sean *hadn't* moved on as well as they'd all thought.

"Should we be worried about him? It's a Monday, for Christ's sake, and The Hut isn't really up to Sean's standards."

"Dude, glass houses."

Max had a point. Noah couldn't criticize Sean for wanting to drown his sorrows when he'd proposed the same damn thing. At least Sean had real, life-altering issues to work through. Angelica was just a blip on the path of Noah's life; he'd probably forget all about her in a couple of months.

At least he was going to try, and drinks at the local dive bar were a good start. After all, he probably wouldn't run into her there. Just because Sean had decided to slum it after years spent in the glitzy clubs and champagne bars of Hollywood didn't mean Angelica could hack it with the rough and tumble inhabitants of River Hill and its surrounding communities.

"So, The Hut at eight then?"

"See you then."

Several hours later, Noah, Max, and Sean were sitting in a line at the rickety bar of The Hut, the grizzled old bartender Harry passing each of them a shot of cheap, bottom shelf whiskey. It burned Noah's throat when he tossed it back, but it did the trick. A few more and he might not care about Angelica at all.

"I'm telling you," he barked, slamming his palm on the sticky bar, "it's only a matter of time until River Hill turns in to Yountville. Or worse, Nob Hill! She's inviting them into our midst."

"Dramatic much?" Sean laughed from the end of the bar.

"I'm not being dramatic," Noah argued, almost tumbling off his stool. Rebalancing himself, he continued, "Remember what happened when Guy Fieri won that food show? He drives a neon-fucking-yellow Ferrari now!"

"Is *that* what you're concerned about?"

"Of course! That car is fucking hideous."

"You're making no sense whatsoever," Max told him. "Angelica isn't like that. She's a nice girl."

"Exactly!" he hollered, triumphantly. "She's a nice girl who likes nice things. Fame is going to go to her head and she's going to start carrying Gucci purses with tiny dogs inside."

"Do you think he even hears what he's saying?" Sean asked Max over Noah's head.

"The better question is do you think he'll remember any of this in the morning?"

"The Diner?" Sean notched his head toward the door.

"Yeah, let's get some coffee in him, otherwise he's going to regret this in the morning."

"The only thing I regret is meeting her," Noah mumbled into his empty shot glass as his two friends hoisted him off the stool and out to Max's car.

It took three mugs of steaming black coffee, two large glasses of ice water, and a heaping serving of scrambled eggs with a mountain-sized side of crispy, greasy bacon before Noah was feeling more like himself.

"Why'd you let me drink that much?" he asked, pushing his plate away with a groan.

"Let you?" Sean asked. "You threatened to punch me when I tried to stop you."

Noah winced and dragged his palms down over his face with undisguised embarrassment. "Fuck, I'm sorry. You know I'd never actually do that, right?

Max smirked. "Yeah, we know. Despite your grumpy disposition, we've known you long enough to realize your bark is worse than your bite."

"Speaking of bark," Noah said, "I should get home

and let Molly out before bed. If I don't, she'll probably shit all over my rug again."

"We still on for Thursday night?" Sean asked, pocketing his change.

"I'm game if you guys are," Max said, looking to Noah for agreement.

"Yeah, I'm in."

"Cool." Sean pushed in his chair and, with his back to his friends, raised his hand in farewell. "See you Thursday."

"You good?" Max asked, concern writ plainly on his face.

"Yeah, I'm good," Noah answered, stretching his back. "Been awhile since I went on a bender like that though."

"You were on a roll," Max said, winding his way toward the diner's exit. "I can't remember the last time I saw you that bent out of shape over a woman."

Noah followed his friend to his car. If he was lucky, once Max dropped him at his truck, he'd be home before midnight. He needed at least five hours of sleep a night to function properly the next day, and he had an important meeting with his vineyard manager at eight to go over some soil readings on the vines that had been planted on Angelica's property.

Angelica.

"Yeah, that woman gets under my skin like no one ever has," he told his friend.

"I kind of got that." Max chuckled, but then sobered. "You had a lot to say about her."

"I was probably talking out my ass."

Max climbed in the driver's seat and turned the ignition. Once Noah slid in next to him, he agreed. "You were. What's your deal anyway?"

Noah's mind flashed to Angelica's naked body pressed up against the tiles of his shower, and the way her thighs had clenched around his head while he pleasured her from his knees. He blinked hard to dislodge the erotic image. "I honestly don't know. I mean, we're fucking—"

"You don't say," Max interrupted.

Noah shot his friend a dirty look and then continued trying to describe his relationship with Angelica. "Sometimes I think she's the most amazing woman I've ever met, and then at other times I want to wring her pretty little neck."

"Like tonight?"

"Yeah, like tonight."

"Anything specific?"

"Ugh. You know how she's doing that renovation show?"

"Yeah, the crew eats at Frankie's at least twice a week."

"Well, today she told me the mayor and the town council want her to film parts of River Hill for the series as well."

"What's wrong with that?" Max asked as he turned down road that would take them back to The Hut and Noah's truck.

Noah groaned. "You know as well as I do how it'll play out."

"More tourists?"

"Exactly."

Max pulled up alongside Noah's Ford and shut off the car. "And how is that bad again?"

He laughed cynically. "Oh, come on. Don't pretend you don't know why I don't want that to happen."

"I don't have to pretend. No matter how I look at it, I can't see the downside. More tourists translates into more money for local businesses. More money equals better services for River Hill. As far as I'm concerned, if Angelica's show puts more butts in the seats at my restaurant, I'm all for it. I honestly don't see a downside."

"Wine buses. Bachelorette parties. People showing up drunk off their faces ten minutes before closing, expecting me to open my most expensive bottles of wine, then spilling it all over and not having the decency to even buy a fucking bottle."

It wasn't hyperbole or a hangover talking. He'd seen it happen at his father's tasting room more than once back when he was younger and still learning the trade. He'd never forgotten the drunk brides who'd thrown themselves at him in an effort to get in one last hurrah before they walked down the aisle. And he'd certainly never forget the one who'd emptied the contents of her stomach all over the bar, splattering vomit all over his shirt. That kind of behavior might fly with other wineries that relied on drunk tourists to pad their bottom line, but he wanted nothing to do with it. He was in it for the sheer joy of creating great wine, and he wanted the people who came to his tasting room to feel that way, too. That was why he'd opened his tasting room in River Hill instead of in one of the larger, more tourist-friendly towns further inland.

But Max wasn't having any of it. "You've got to be kidding."

"I assure you, I'm not."

"You do realize you don't have to open your winery up to buses and large parties just because River Hill might get its fifteen minutes of fame, right?"

When he didn't answer, Max pressed further. "Given your silence, I'm guessing there's something else you're not saying."

Noah stewed on it for a few moments. While he hated to imagine his winery turning into a carbon copy of his father's, Max was right. He bristled at the idea of River Hill being overrun with tourists and his favorite haunts being changed to accommodate them, but that might happen even without Angelica's show. The truth was, no wine country town was immune to that possibility.

So what was his problem then?

His conversation with Angelica kept coming back to him—specifically, three little words she'd uttered. *My personal brand.*

Logically, he knew she'd need to establish her B&B through word of mouth and travel sites for it to be successful. He wasn't opposed to that. But Noah had dated a few women who didn't care what their actual lives were like so long as their online presence showed something that was perfect and enviable. *Their brands,* they'd all called it. In that world, likes and hearts equaled endorsements and sponsorship opportunities that were more important than actual conversations and shared interests. Everyone was your friend when no one really was. He wanted nothing to do with any of it.

The most disappointing part of this was he hadn't pegged Angelica for one of them. Maybe he'd been wrong though. And if he was, soon she'd try to cash in on his family's name, too. It had happened more times than he could count over the years.

Aside from Naomi, he couldn't name one woman he'd been involved with who hadn't wanted to boast about the famous Blackstone name to push her own self-interests. And that's what had him most on edge, he realized. He'd run far away from San Francisco to get away from women like that. River Hill was supposed to be his safe place, where he could lead the type of life he wanted, away from everything he'd turned his back on.

But this wasn't a conversation he was going to have with Max. At least not yet. First, he needed to talk to Angelica and make sure she knew, in no uncertain terms, that he was not for sale. His name was not for sale. And if she thought it was, they were through. No sex—no matter how magnificent—was worth his pride.

Noah pushed open the door and unbuckled his belt.

"Nope, that's it," he said, climbing out and shutting the door.

$\mathcal{N}$oah clipped Molly's leash to the shelf inside his mudroom and went to lock up when he spied Angelica's kitchen light glowing across the field like a beacon in the pitch black. Checking his watch, he saw it was nearly midnight. He should go upstairs to bed, but that yellow orb—and the woman inside—beckoned to him like a siren. He shrugged back into his coat and locked the back door.

When he reached Angelica's porch, his heart was racing, but it wasn't from the brisk walk through the vines and up her long drive. He had so much to say, but he didn't know where to begin.

Before he could put his thoughts in order, Angelica opened the door, her perfect curves illuminated by the soft, warm glow from the lamp a few feet behind her.

"Noah?" She clutched the sides of her faded terry cloth robe closed around her middle.

Dragging his eyes away from the soft mounds of her unbound breasts, he swallowed. "We need to talk."

"It's the middle of the night."

"And yet we're both awake."

"I was going back up to bed. I only came down for some water."

"I won't keep you," he said. He needed to get this over with; just say what he'd come to say. Because the longer he was in Angelica's presence, the harder it was to remember his earlier convictions. "Can I come in?"

Her brows drew down in confusion, but she moved aside to let him enter.

Noah stepped over the threshold. The door closed behind him and when he turned, she was leaning back against it, her palms flat on the wood. "You look upset."

"I'm not upset," he said, more forcefully than he'd intended. Wordlessly, she tipped her head toward his clenched fists. Okay, maybe he *was* upset. Loosening his fingers, he repeated his earlier statement. "We need to talk."

"So talk."

Without conscious thought, he took a step toward her. "I don't want you to film the Harvest Festival for your show."

Her chin jutted forward, and she crossed her arms over her chest. "I really don't think that's up to you."

Noah huffed. "I figured you'd say that."

"Then why bother coming here?" she asked, pushing off the door and taking a step forward.

He took two steps closer. "Because I needed to see if I was right."

"And were you?"

He didn't answer right away because his eyes were glued to her chest, which was rising and falling with rapid breaths that were probably fueled by barely-suppressed rage.

"Hey! I'm up here."

Without shame, he took in her bounty, the soft

peaks and valleys he knew by heart, until his eyes swept upward to meet her glare. "Yeah, but for how much longer?"

Her head snapped back. She breathed in deeply, twice, then took a step forward until they were close enough that Noah could smell the faint scent of her toothpaste with each exhalation. "What the hell does that mean?"

He reached out and brushed her hair off her shoulder. "Exactly what you think it means. What's your endgame here, Angelica?"

She planted her small hands on his chest as if she was going to push him away, but then her fingers tangled in his shirt and she pulled him even closer. "I sank every dollar I have into this house. It's my *home*. And River Hill is my home too, whether you like it or not."

"Good answer," he murmured, his lips hovering over hers.

"Was that some sort of test?"

"I don't know," he said, his nose brushing against her petal soft skin. She smelled like jasmine and honey, and suddenly he didn't care about this conversation anymore. He wanted to devour her. "Angelica?"

"Yes?" she breathed out, the pulse point in her neck bouncing rapidly.

"Are you as turned on as I am right now?"

She chuckled, a rich, seductive sound, and her tongue darted out to lick a quick path over his lips. "I don't know. Do you want me so bad you can't stop thinking about ripping my clothes off and fucking me against this door?" Her hand dropped from his shirt to the uncomfortable bulge in his jeans. She cupped him and squeezed. "Do you want it so hard and fast that you still feel me on your skin in the morning?"

In three long strides, he backed her against the door. "Fuck yes," he growled against her lips, claiming them in a searing kiss, all his anger, frustration, and desire for this woman spilling forth.

Angelica ripped her mouth away. She captured his gaze as she undid his pants and pulled his cock free. "Then do it, Noah. Fuck me like you mean it."

Splitting the panels of her robe, he gripped the globes of her ass and hefted her up around his hips. When her legs were wrapped tight around his waist, he drove into her hard and unforgiving. Just like she'd told him to. And when she came screaming his name, he followed her over the edge, his vision blurring and his legs shaking.

Slowly, he set her down on her feet. When he slid from her wet heat he realized they hadn't used protection. "Shit, we didn't use a condom." His eyes swung to her's uncertainly. He was a fucking asshole. There was no excuse for what he'd just done. None, except for the fact that she made him crazy and when he was near her, he lost his goddamn mind.

"It's okay." She sucked in a breath and exhaled slowly before adding, "I have an IUD."

He nodded, accepting her word as truth. He might have a number of conflicting thoughts banging around in his head about her, but he knew Angelica wasn't a liar.

"I'm clean," he offered, guilt gnawing at his belly. He hadn't gone bare since one stupid night in college. It was no wonder he'd nearly passed out when her walls had gripped him tight and she'd fluttered her completion along his dick.

Angelica nodded and righted her robe. Stepping to the side, she tied the sash in a tight knot and smoothed her hands down the front of the fabric. "I think you should leave now," she said, gripping the door handle and twisting it open. "We've both said enough for one night."

Noah didn't argue. How could he? Instead, he raised her chin so she'd meet his eyes. "I'll go, but this isn't over."

Her eyes flicked between his and her mouth turned down in a frown. "No, I don't expect it is."

That night, for all the tumult of his day, Noah slept the sleep of the dead, and when his alarm went off at dawn, the world didn't seem quite as bleak as it had before. He wouldn't go so far as to say a good hard fuck had solved their problems, but the way he'd felt when he'd emptied himself inside Angelica had certainly clarified a few things for him. The most surprising being that he might care about her almost as much as he did his beloved River Hill.

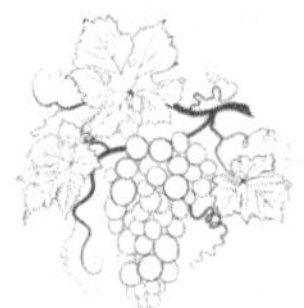

CHAPTER FOURTEEN

"Ugh. I hate these things." Angelica fidgeted, smoothing invisible wrinkles out of the sparkling gold fabric of her borrowed dress.

Gold to make the advertisers think of money, Leah had said with a laugh when she'd brought it over the day before. Leah had a friend who created the costumes for a TV show set in high society, and the network's budget was big enough that she didn't have to scrimp on quality. Conveniently, Angelica happened to be the same size as the actress who played the villainess, something she preferred not to think about. All of the "good" characters wore a size two, of course.

Angelica had never been a big enough name to have designers clamoring to dress her. And once she'd stopped starving herself to fit into sample sizes, she'd entered into an unspoken agreement with the fashion gods: she and high couture each politely pretended the other didn't exist. When she'd officially retired from acting, she'd held a little ceremony where she'd burned the business cards from designers' assistants she'd been collecting for years. It had felt good. Jai had been horrified, of course. She didn't regret it, even though he'd been right in one respect: she did still need dresses occasionally. But she much preferred relying on the kindness of her friends—or to shell out her own money—than to beg for crumbs from snobby fashion folk.

"I love these things," Jai said, glancing around. "Look, tiny sandwiches!"

"You're just lucky I needed a date," Angelica grumbled. "Greg would never have come with you to this thing."

Her agent patted her arm. "That's why I'm married to him, and not you, darling. He has other compatible interests. And he doesn't complain nearly as much."

"Can't argue with you there." Greg was a saint. How Jai had landed the shy architect was beyond her, and how the couple had stayed together for more than ten years was something she'd always envied. "It's a good thing you have me. Wouldn't want you to lose your edge over a lack of complaining in your life. Witty retorts are kind of your thing."

Jai snorted as they made their way to a good vantage point for people watching. "Trust me, sugar, I'll never experience a lack of complaining in this industry."

Jai's client list ranged from ditzy to diva, and Angelica liked to think she was somewhere in the middle. He managed the entire roster with effortless ease, making him increasingly in demand. She was lucky to still have him, to be honest.

"Okay, tell me the plan." She forced her hands away from her waist. The dress fit perfectly. No adjusting needed. She tucked her hands around Jai's elbow to force herself to stop fidgeting and looked into his eyes inquiringly.

"Very nice." He patted her arm. "These old white men are going to eat you up."

She shuddered. "I'd really rather they didn't."

"Yes, I heard you've been busy being devoured by somebody else." Jai grinned. "No secrets, Ang."

She swallowed uncomfortably. She hadn't talked to Noah since he'd come over to inexplicably yell at her and they'd wound up having sex instead. She'd meant to call him, but there'd been six different electrical problems and a countertop disaster to solve, plus filming and a promotional appearance. And it wasn't like he'd called her either. The sex had been incredible —she could feel herself warming just thinking about it —but it hadn't solved whatever bug he'd gotten up his ass about the Harvest Festival.

"It's just sex," she said, waving away Jai's speculative grin.

He raised an eyebrow. "With that lumberjack who lives next door?"

"He grows grapes, Jai. Just because he wears flannel shirts doesn't mean he cuts down trees for a living."

He sniffed. "I'll take your word for it. So why isn't

the not-lumberjack on your arm? Not that I don't appreciate the opportunity." He reached out with casual elegance and snagged two glasses of champagne from a passing waiter.

Angelica took one. "Why would he be?"

"No reason." He side-eyed her over the rim of his glass as he sipped. "I mean, I know I'm beautiful, but if you wanted arm candy—"

"I'm here professionally, not for fun," Angelica said sharply. "I don't need arm candy. Can we please talk about what we're doing tonight instead?"

"Fine." Jai nodded toward a group of men in sharply tailored suits who were being circled lazily by women in misty chiffon gowns that emphasized their youth. "Group one. Producers."

"No, thanks." Angelica shook her head. "I'm putting all my eggs in one basket, Jai. I don't want to cozy up to anybody for future work. Just this one show."

Her agent sighed. "Fine. Stay away from them, then. They're terrible." He tilted his glass toward several groups in succession, champagne sloshing but not spilling. "Car companies. Luxury winemakers. High-end fashion CEOs." He squinted. "I think that's the president of a cruise line. Take your pick."

Angelica made a face. "You know, every time I attend one of these things, I feel like I'm being sucked back in." She held her fingers near her mouth and wiggled them like tentacles while she made her best attempt at sucking noises.

"Will you please stop before somebody with money

sees you?" His tone was fond but exasperated. "And may I remind you that the life you find so awful pays both my bills and yours?"

"I wish you wouldn't. I like to exist in blissful ignorance."

"Well, put on your blissfullest face and go make nice with some of these advertisers," Jai said. "Who'll it be?"

Angelica sighed. "Car companies first, I guess."

"Give it a little shimmy," Jai called after her as she strode toward her first target. "Pretend you're in a leather seat."

Three CEOs later, Angelica was starting to feel worn out and lacking in the charm department. She hated the hustle. She'd always enjoyed the acting part of her career and getting to know the technical teams behind the filming process, but the business end had never been her thing.

At least fake-flirting with businessmen at a charity gala was less dangerous than auditioning for producers in their hotel rooms. She'd heard far too many horror stories from other actresses about truly awful men doing really terrible things in the name of "helping" with their careers. The worst she had ever experienced was a few unwanted gropings and a number of suggestive comments, but then, she'd never aimed for superstardom. Apparently, when you built a career on secondary roles, you flew mostly under the radar. Which was fine by her.

These particular advertisers seemed perfectly okay with her level of fame, though. She'd smiled her way through descriptions of the show and effusive praise of the network, then complimented the wives and made a point of emphasizing River Hill's many charms. She'd extracted several promises to contact the network for advertising space. In the few hours she'd been at it, she'd definitely earned her keep. She deserved a break, and there was a tiny sandwich somewhere with her name on it.

She hadn't seen Jai since they'd parted ways, but she suspected he was somewhere in the producers' orbit, reminding them of the many talented faces he had under his purview. He might pretend he was there as her date, but he was working, too.

Angelica found a pitcher of cucumber-infused water and poured herself a glass, sipping gratefully as she enjoyed not talking for a few minutes. She was scanning the nearby food stations and wishing Frankie's catered events like this when she heard her name called in a surprised tone.

"Angelica?" The voice was familiar, but when she turned around, all she saw was a beautiful brunette she didn't recognize on the arm of a tall, dark, and handsome man in an impeccably tailored suit. Even his shoes were expensive. Jai would be drooling over the stitching detail on the shiny ebony leather. Her eyes traveled up, her brain fighting with realization. The height was right, and the voice was right, and the hair was … well, it was far tamer than she'd ever seen it. How could it be? And here, of all places?

"Noah?" she asked, her voice coming out as a perplexed squeak.

He was barely recognizable. The suit—and the brunette—made him fit right in, a seamless part of the crowd of rich businessmen and society people. She gulped. "I … I didn't recognize you?" Why had it come out sounding like a question?

"What are you doing here?" Meanwhile, his tone was faintly accusing, and she went straight from unnerved to annoyed—as usual.

"I'm working. What are *you* doing here?" She met the gaze of the woman on his arm, who was more amused than Angelica preferred.

Noah frowned. "I'm here because my mother asked me to be." He nodded in the direction of an elegantly dressed woman near the bar, and Angelica followed his gaze.

Wait, wasn't that the chairwoman of the gala? Jai had pointed her out when they'd arrived. Her name was Ber-something. Angelica searched the catalog of names she'd stashed away throughout the night. Bernice, yes that was it. Bernice … Bradstone, she realized with dread.

"Wait, your mother is—"

"—Are you telling me you honestly had no idea who I am?" he interrupted.

She frowned at him, her eyebrows furrowing into a

deep vee. If Jai saw her, he'd freak and warn her about the dangers of Botox. "Are you somebody important?"

The woman beside him started to laugh. "Only in his own mind," she said, and Noah scowled at her.

"How is that helpful?" he snapped.

"Oh, I'm not here to be helpful," the woman said.

Angelica was starting to like her, much as she didn't want to. "I'm Angelica Travis," she said pointedly, since Noah didn't seem inclined to make introductions.

At least he had the grace to look embarrassed. "This is—"

"—Naomi Klein," the woman said, extending her hand. "It's nice to meet you, finally."

"Finally?" Angelica looked to Noah, who just shrugged.

"I've known Noah for years," Naomi explained. "I live in River Hill too, actually."

Angelica stared at Noah. Nothing about this conversation made him come off in a positive light. "Really."

Naomi grinned. "Feel free to eviscerate him if you want, but it's not like that. We've known each other since we were kids. My family and his are close."

There was that mention of his family again. Angelica held up her hands to signal a timeout. "Can I just get a quick update, here?" She was clearly missing some important information that Noah assumed she'd already had.

Angelica looked at Naomi, assuming the other

woman would tell her the truth. "What's the deal with his family?"

"They're rich," Naomi said cheerfully. "Disgustingly so. His father is Carter Bradstone." She raised an eyebrow at Angelica, who shook her head. The name meant nothing to her. "Big name in wine. Like, huge."

Angelica looked back at Noah. "So, you're following in your father's footsteps?"

"I'm trying to step out of them, actually," he said. "My parents love this scene." He waved a hand to indicate the sparkling festivities around them. "I just want to make really good wine and push the industry forward with innovative techniques. My dad's not into it."

"And my family is, shall we say, moderately unsupportive of my career, too," Naomi added. At Angelica's blank look, she explained. "I'm an artist. A sculptor, actually, though I do some graphic design to pay bills."

"She does my labels," Noah said.

"My dad hated the one with the half-naked woman," Naomi added with relish.

"I thought it was very tasteful," he protested.

"You and the disapproving Dr. Klein disagree about a lot of things."

Their banter was quick, and Angelica didn't have a place in it. And she wasn't entirely sure she wanted one. Naomi seemed nice, but she was here with Noah. Which only served to underscore that he wasn't there with *her*.

Jai's words echoed in her head. *If you want arm candy...*

It honestly hadn't occurred to her to ask Noah if he wanted to come with her. She'd assumed he'd feel out of place at an event like this. He was so committed to life in River Hill that he'd blown up at her for just wanting to film the Harvest Festival. Not exactly the sort of man she expected to be lurking about a society gala in an impeccable tux, fitting right in with all the sleek trophy wives, CEOs, and politicians.

So which was the real Noah? Angelica had thought they were getting to know one another, but between their last argument and now this? She suddenly realized she didn't really know him at all.

Completely flustered, she did the only thing she could think of—flee. "I, uh, think I see a … an advertiser," she improvised. "Better go talk to them about the show." She hot-footed away from Noah and Naomi as quickly as she could without tripping over her gown.

She needed time to think. And something to drink.

CHAPTER FIFTEEN

"So that's Angelica?" Naomi's eyes followed the other woman's hasty retreat, brows furrowed with concern. "She's lovely. And very much surprised to see you here."

"Yeah." Noah scrubbed a hand over his chin, his eyes glued to Angelica's curves as she walked away from him. He couldn't help but admire how well she filled out her gown. The fact that he knew exactly what she looked like underneath it had him imagining all the ways he'd love to strip her out of it later. Except, he told himself, they weren't going to do that anymore. "All that's over with. She's not who I thought she was."

"Who you thought she was, or who you wanted her to be?" Naomi pointed an accusing finger in his direction.

"She told me she was done with Hollywood, and everything that went along with it."

"And?" Naomi crossed her arms and tapped the ball

of her four-inch heeled foot, somehow managing to still look elegant despite the spikes that would have toppled a lesser woman.

"And," he said with a sigh, "I don't want to get involved with someone who's more concerned about their fans and social media followers than their friends and the community."

Naomi scoffed. "I seriously doubt that woman gives two shits about all that. She left Hollywood for a normal life, or have you forgotten?"

"And the second they came knocking at her broken-down, dilapidated door, she opened up and welcomed them back in with open arms," Noah countered, his voice rising in agitation.

"So what if she did? That doesn't mean anything except she's a single woman with a huge mortgage, mounting bills to restore that property, and the means to do so using her connections. Would you seriously deny her that?'

Was it just him, or had someone turned up the temperature in the room? He fingered the collar of his shirt. "That's not fair. Of course I want her to succeed."

She shot him a glance there was no mistaking. Naomi wasn't buying it for a second. "As long as you get to be the big, bad man and she's the little woman?"

"No! Of course not. What are you even talking about?"

"I'm talking about the fact that while you're a lovely, wonderful man, you're also a bit of a chauvinist, Noah Bradstone."

Sweat prickling his brow now, he replied, "I am not a chauvinist. What's your problem? I thought you were on my side."

"Oh, Noah," Naomi sighed. "I'm *always* on your side. And that means when you're behaving like an ass, I'm going to call you on it. And right now, I think there's a little bit of Neanderthal in you."

Wordlessly, he tugged on his expertly knotted tie. He suddenly felt like he was choking.

Naomi swatted at his hand and took over adjusting the navy blue silk. "Angelica is wonderful, but you're scared of what you feel for her, so you're pulling out every damn excuse you can think of why you should stay away. First it was the situation with the vines. Then it was the fact that she's your neighbor. Now it's the TV show."

She must be wrong, he thought. But then he remembered that Max and Sean had said something similar the weekend before, and he was forced to acknowledge he might be self-sabotaging. He just couldn't figure out why.

"There, all better," she said, leaning in for a quick hug. Noah's arms automatically circled her waist. With her cheek resting against his chest, she said, "Max told me your theory about the tourists and frankly, I think you're being selfish." She leaned away and serious eyes locked on his. "That show filming in River Hill is a *good* thing, Noah. It benefits so many people. But more importantly, it benefits Angelica. We want her to be happy there. We want her to stay."

"Why?" he asked. "You don't even know her."

She smiled warmly. "Because *you* want it, silly. You just don't know it yet." She eyed him speculatively for a few moments. "Although maybe you're beginning to figure it out."

Maybe he was.

Because if Noah took a step back and examined why he was so against her filming the festival, none of his objections actually made any sense. Sure, he didn't want to be part of the show, but then she hadn't asked him to. He'd just automatically assumed she was going to; that she'd use him the way so many others had tried before.

Logically, he knew the show's short-term success would mean Angelica's bed and breakfast's long-term success, but that whole thing about building her brand still niggled at him. He wanted Angelica to be above all that. But even if she wasn't, did that mean they couldn't be together? Was it something he could look beyond? Did he care more about that exasperating, beautiful, magical woman than he cared about his hatred for social media?

Naomi had certainly given him something to think about.

He pulled her back to him and squeezed tight. "Thank you," he said to the top of her head. "You're right, I'm an asshole. I need to go make things right with her."

He let go of his friend and was about to leave to find Angelica when his mother approached. Her eyes zeroed in on his and Naomi's close proximity and they flashed with a satisfied gleam. He took a large step back, but it was too late.

"Well, isn't this cozy?" His mother leaned in to place an air kiss on Naomi's cheek. "Lovely to see you again, dear. Don't you look stunning? You're the most beautiful young lady in the room tonight, I'd wager."

"Thank you, Mrs. Bradstone. While I appreciate the sentiment, I'm not sure I agree." Her eyes searched the room and landed on Angelica, who was embroiled in what looked like a heated discussion with a dark, handsome man who was at least six inches shorter than she was. "I think that honor goes to Angelica Travis over there." Naomi tipped her chin toward the other side of the room, and Bernice's eyes followed.

"Oh my," she murmured. "She is beautiful, isn't she?" Noah's chest swelled with pride, but then his mother turned back to them and ruined the moment entirely. "It's a shame about her weight though. Imagine if she were thirty pounds lighter? She'd be stunning."

His heart kicked with rage, but he pushed his reaction deep down where it wouldn't see the light of day. Pulling in a breath to calm himself, he held it for several beats and then exhaled slowly. He didn't want to say something he might regret later. Not that he'd regret setting his mother straight; he'd only regret having to deal with her antics for the next month. Her narrow-minded way of thinking about a person's worth was one reason he'd stayed far away from the her social circle. They were uniformly the most vapid, soulless creatures he'd ever met. Frankly, he often thought a lot of that had to do with being in a constant state of hunger.

With that, his mind flashed to the meal he and Angelica had shared on his back deck. Specifically, how she'd gleefully devoured her steak, and the seductive way her lush, full lips had circled the fork when he'd fed her a bite of Max's sinfully caloric potatoes. And the way she'd fed him back.

Stifling a groan, he adjusted his stance to disguise his thickening cock and cleared his throat. Despite the impending fallout from correcting his mother, he fully intended to say something, but Naomi stayed him with a hand to his arm and a quick shake of her head.

"Actually, I think she's amazing," she said before he could speak. Then she looked ruefully down the length of her own trim body, honed to slim perfection through hours of yoga and pilates. "I would kill for an ounce of her curves."

Bernice's eyes flashed with momentary surprise, but then she masked her reaction. "Oh, no dear, you're perfect as you are. Isn't she Noah?" His mother's tone was clear: *don't you dare contradict me.*

He smiled affectionately at Naomi. "Of course she's perfect, but I have to agree with her earlier assessment of Miss Travis."

"Hey!" Naomi said with a playful slap on his arm. "None of that now."

Noah winked, then turned to find his mother

eyeing them curiously, as if she knew something was about to happen but she had no clue what. *I can't wait to see the look on her face*, Noah thought, before saying with relish, "What I mean is, I would kill for an ounce of Angelica's curves myself."

His mother's mouth fell open and then closed in shock, while Naomi laughed uproariously. Pushing him away, she said, "Then you better go get a move on."

*N*oah's eyes scanned the ornately decorated space, seeking out the object of his desire. A few times he spotted a flash of liquid gold moving through the crowd, but each time it had been someone else. Resigning himself to not finding Angelica in the swelling crowd, he gave up and told Naomi he was heading home—not to his pied-à-terre in SoMA, but to his *real* home. Back to River Hill. She'd kissed him on both cheeks and wished him well before returning to the side of an older man who'd just commissioned a sculpture for his home in Palo Alto.

Buttoning his coat, Noah stepped into the foyer to find the elevator clanking shut. "Hold the door!" he called, rushing forward. He shoved his hands between the old-fashioned sliding brass bars, slipped into the ten-by-ten box, and came to a sudden stop. "Angelica," he breathed. "Finally."

Her eyes raked over him, and not with appreciation the way they usually did. "Hello, Noah."

The antique elevator lurched and started moving. Setting his hand on the shiny bar skirting the perimeter, he took a step closer. "I've been looking everywhere for you."

She raised a skeptical eyebrow. "Really? It looked to me like you were just fine where you were."

"Naomi and I are old friends. She told you that."

"Right. Old, *close* friends."

He didn't mistake the hurt in her eyes, but he wasn't going to lie to her either. "Yes, we're close."

"Like you and I've been close?" she asked, as the elevator lurched to a stop and she stumbled into his arms.

"What the?" he exclaimed, catching her and planting his feet before they both tumbled to the ground. Setting her away, he turned to the electrical panel and muttered, "You have got to be kidding me."

"I'm sorry," she responded from behind, her voice filled with frost.

Noah looked at her over his shoulder. "Sorry, that wasn't about you. I love it when you throw yourself at me," he said with a wink. "I was talking about this damn elevator." He brought his face back around and stared at the buttons in front of him. Every single one of them was lit up and blinking.

He took off his wool overcoat and set it lengthwise on the floor. Dropping down onto it, he patted the space next to him. "You better get comfortable. We're going to be here awhile."

Angelica jutted out her chin. "I'll stand, thank you."

Noah decided not to force the issue. She was wearing impossibly high heels; it was only a matter of time until they'd start to pinch and she'd join him down there. He shrugged. "Suit yourself. But like I said, we're going to be here awhile."

"How do you know that?" she asked distrustfully, balancing on the ball of one foot and then the other.

Yeah, she'd be joining him *very soon*, he thought with an inward chuckle.

"Would you believe it if I told you this was the third time this has happened to me?"

"You're kidding."

"Nope," he said, his lips popping on the p. "A bunch of us got trapped in here during Naomi's bat mitzvah. And then again when I was leaving a wedding a few years back. That time, I was alone, and as you'll soon learn, there's no cell reception in here. God, that sucked." He shook his head. "I don't know why people keep having events up here when this shit happens all the damn time. They never fix it."

Angelica's throat bobbed with a deep swallow. "How long were you stuck?"

Noah scrunched up his face, trying to remember back to Naomi's thirteenth birthday. "The first time, maybe an hour or two. There were six of us, and being idiot kids, we thought it was a grand old time. Naomi was pissed because she was missing her party, but the rest of us decided to use our time wisely to play spin the paperclip."

"Spin the paperclip?"

He smiled wolfishly. "In the absence of a bottle, we got creative. Someone had one in their pockets."

She nodded, but Noah noticed the color had drained from her face. "And the second time?"

If she didn't like his first answer, she was really going to hate this one. "Four hours."

She blew out a breath and her knees buckled before she caught herself. "Four hours?"

He nodded. "And I was alone, with nobody to talk to. At least this time I have you."

Angelica closed her eyes and slid down the length of the wall until she was sitting on the floor across from him.

"Come sit with me," he said coaxingly. "You're going to ruin your dress."

Angelica shook her head.

"Why not?"

"Because I'm mad at you."

"Can I ask why?"

Her eyes slid open and she fixed him with an unreadable look. "Because you lied to me."

That wasn't the answer he'd expected. Frankly, he'd been prepared for her to say something more about his friendship with Naomi. "When did I lie to you?"

She blew out a long breath. "You didn't lie outright, I guess, but you weren't very truthful with me either. We've spent hours together, and you never once told me about *this* Noah." She flicked her wrist up and down between them. "I thought you were this small town, salt-of-the-earth man who was more farmer than … whatever—*whoever*—you are tonight."

"I *am* a small town, salt-of-the-earth kind of guy," he protested.

She raised a skeptical eyebrow. "And yet here we are."

"And yet here we are," he agreed slowly. "But I didn't *want* to be here tonight. I would have given anything to be sitting on my deck, sipping a beer with Molly at my feet. But yes, I also come from this world. My mom is … well, let's just say in the San Francisco socialite pecking order, she's at the top of the heap."

"And you never thought to mention you had this whole other life."

He stared at her a few beats. "No, I didn't."

"Why?"

It was his turn to blow out a frustrated breath. "For a long time, there've been expectations placed on me. From my mother, her friends, their daughters. Pretty much every woman except Naomi. Since I was eighteen, they've all wanted a piece of me. Over the years, I dated a few of them, but it was always the same thing. None of them cared what my interests are, what I wanted out of life. All they cared about was the size of my trust fund and the name on my birth certificate. To them, I'm not Noah Bradstone, winemaker; I'm Noah Bradstone, social stepping stone."

Angelica's eyes flashed with sympathy, but then cooled. "I'm sorry you've experienced that, but that's not me. And I've done nothing to give you the impression that I am."

"Except here you are."

Her eyes sparked with indignation. "Working," she said from between clenched teeth. "I'm here because my producers need more advertisers. Their ad department can't muster up the right sort of sponsorships, so they poured me into this dress and sent me along as bait instead. If I had my way, I'd be at home bundled in a robe, drinking a glass of wine, and painting my toenails while watching a *Scandal* marathon." She crossed her arms over her chest and rubbed her hands over her exposed arms.

"Are you cold?"

She shook her head and gave him her profile. "No."

Since the goose pimples dotting her skin told a different tale, he gathered his coat and moved to her side. "Liar," he said, draping the expensive wool over her shoulders.

Angelica didn't respond to his taunt. Instead, a few tense moments passed between them until she asked, "Why didn't you ask me to come with you tonight?"

He sighed, and wrapped his arm around her shoulder. Pulling her flush against him, he kissed the top of her head. "I should have, but I've been confused about some things."

"What sort of things?" she asked, shifting to rest her cheek against him.

"Things about you and me. About how I feel about you." He chuckled. "You know you make me crazy."

She harrumphed. "I make you grumpy."

"Nah, I'm always grumpy." Noah smiled and reached down to lift Angelica's chin so their mouths were only inches apart. "But you do something to me I can't explain. From the very first moment we met, I haven't been able to control myself around you." He dropped his head closer so their lips were almost touching. "You make me burn, Angelica."

He kissed her then, and when she opened to him and their tongues tangled, he couldn't remember why they hadn't been doing this every single day. Every single hour.

When Angelica's arms came around his neck, he groaned into her mouth and took the kiss deeper. His hands roamed the contours of her body, the thin silk slipping and sliding over her skin. And when he eased her onto her back, she went willingly with a sigh of longing.

"I want you," he told her, nipping at the spot where her neck met her collarbone. "Please, let me have you. I need to be inside of you."

When her thighs slid open in invitation, Noah skated his hand up under her dress to find her bare and ready for him. "You're not wearing underwear."

She giggled, and then gasped, when he slipped a finger inside. "Not in this dress," she croaked, when that finger twisted and curved exactly how she liked.

"I fucking love this dress," he said moments before claiming her mouth again.

Angelica reached between them to undo his belt

and lower his zipper. And then her hand circled his aching cock and she pulled him free. "I want you too," she said, guiding him to her entrance.

Noah levered his body over hers, and then pushed in halfway and held still, luxuriating in the feel of her gripping him tight. When Angelica canted her hips and begged for more, he happily obliged. Sheathing himself to the root in one fluid stroke, he said, "I never want to be anywhere else." He pulled all the way out and then slid home again.

"I never want you anywhere else either," she panted as she ground up against his pelvis. "You feel so good."

"You feel like heaven," he sighed with another thrust.

Angelica's eyes screwed shut and she arched her back. This time, when her body broke out in goose pimples, Noah knew it wasn't because she was cold.

And neither was he. He hadn't lied before; he was burning up for this woman. "I'm going to come," he said against her mouth as he got ready to pull out.

She dropped her hands to his ass and pulled him close. "In me," she said. "I want all of you."

And so he gave her every piece of himself, including his heart.

Forty minutes later when they were rescued, Noah couldn't help but feel disappointed. He knew it was wrong, but he'd been hoping they'd have hours alone together so they could talk. They'd only scratched the surface of what needed to be said.

Stepping out onto the sidewalk side-by-side, Angelica looked up at him uncertainly. "Now what?"

He pulled her against him. "Come home with me tonight."

She chewed her lip. "I would, but I got a room. All my stuff is there."

He looked out over the street, still full of cars at nearly midnight. "Where?"

"At the Courtyard Marriott in Union Square." She dropped her eyes and looked away.

"Hey," he said, touching her chin lightly to pull it up so their eyes met. "What's that all about?"

"I'd invite you back, but you know." She shrugged.

No, he didn't. "Know what?"

"It's not exactly the St. Regis," she answered.

"The St. Regis?" And then he understood. The money thing.

"The producers didn't spring for a hotel, but I didn't want to have to drive home tonight exhausted, so I booked my own room. I'm on a budget, so I went with something cheap. You're probably used to staying somewhere really nice. And expensive. And that's not the Courtyard." Abruptly, she quit talking and her eyes went wide with worry. "Sorry, I babble when I'm nervous."

"Why are you nervous?"

She shook her head. "I don't know. I guess I'm still

weirded out about this whole thing. I thought I was fall
—" she quickly cleared her throat "—getting to know
one man, and now I find out there's a whole other side
of him I hadn't counted on."

He chuckled. "That's what relationships are about
though, aren't they? Learning all about a person,
knowing what makes them tick, who they are in the
best and worst-case scenarios."

She peered up at him from lowered lashes. "Is that
what this is? A relationship?"

Noah swallowed. He'd never intended to fall for
this woman, and yet tonight he finally realized that he
had. He'd fallen hard, fast, and deep, and he hoped she
felt even an inkling of the same way about him. "It can
be, if you want." Friends with benefits would never be
enough for him now.

Angelica took a step back and he let her go.

That wasn't a good sign.

She put her hand to her forehand and scanned the
sidewalk. Then she touched her palm to her cheek and
laughed nervously. Her eyes flicked between his, and
he saw a question there, but still she didn't speak.

Shit, that was a *terrible* sign.

His self-preservation instincts kicked in and he
took a step back. "Forget it. It was a silly thing to say."

Angelica took a step forward. "It's not silly, it's just
…"

"Just what?"

"Unexpected," she answered. "We talked about this.
Friends with benefits. I thought that's all you wanted."

He ran a rough hand through his hair. "I thought that's what I wanted, too, but tonight changed something for me. In the elevator earlier, I meant what I said."

Angelica's face softened, and her eyes went hazy. "Can you give me a couple of days to think about it?"

He swallowed and bit his tongue. He wanted to tell her to take it or leave it—to take *him* or leave him. He wasn't used to women turning him down, and the longer this conversation lasted, the worse his pride fared.

This isn't about your pride, he chided himself. It was about building something lasting with Angelica. He needed to swallow his pride. He shoved his hands in his pockets. "Sure. Take all the time you need." He took a step back, and then another.

She shrugged out of his coat and held it out. "Here, your jacket."

Noah reached his arm out and a taxi crossed two lanes of traffic to pull up next to him. He opened the door and stepped aside. "Keep it."

"Are you sure?" she asked, taking a half step forward.

"Absolutely." He gestured toward the open door of the waiting cab. "Your chariot awaits."

"I can walk," she answered, even as she took a few halting steps toward the waiting vehicle.

Noah chuckled. "Not in those shoes, you can't. But even if you were in flats, I'd still put you in a cab."

"Okay, if you insist." Angelica brushed past him and

slid into the empty back seat. Leaning forward so their eyes connected, she asked, "Are we okay?"

He smiled down at her. "We will be."

And then he closed the door, smacked the roof of the taxi, and waved as the car pulled away from the curb.

CHAPTER SIXTEEN

*H*e wants a relationship. Angelica turned the words over in her head as she tossed and turned in her hotel bed that night, the sheets sliding uncomfortably along her skin as she remembered the hot, eager sensation of Noah's hands and lips on her body.

The r-word continued burning its way through her brain hours later while she gulped down her mediocre continental breakfast, scalding the roof of her mouth with terrible coffee.

And it didn't go away as she had her hair and makeup done for the day, nor as she ruined Leah's work by scraping away layers of grime from the grout of the third guest bathroom on camera. When she rubbed the grit out of her eyebrows, she swore she heard it whisper *relationshiiiiiiiip* as it fell into the sink.

Later, she held up wood stain samples to compare them to the original wood floor of the second bedroom, where they'd had to put in a patch of new wood to replace a rotting section. Noah's face looked back at her from the empty air between the pieces of wood, and she put them down hastily.

She heard a tiny beep and turned to Roger, who was frowning at her from next to a camera.

"What's wrong with you?" He was nothing if not blunt.

"What do you mean?" She glanced at the camera. The little red 'recording' light was off. The beep she'd heard had been Roger powering the unit down.

"You're a thousand miles away, Angelica. And you're not giving good face."

She could feel herself blanching. "I'm not—" she started to argue, but it was no use because he wouldn't let her bullshit her way out of what she knew to be true.

"You're *not*." His tone was firm. "I'm not trying to be a dick, but get it together." He gathered up a few cables in one arm and used the other hand to flip his baseball cap from backwards to forwards, a sign he wouldn't be looking into the viewscreen anytime soon. "Let's take a break."

"I don't need—"

He held up a hand. "You *do* need a break, and so does everyone else." He paused, and Angelica thought he looked uncomfortable. "Do you … want me to get Leah? To, I don't know, talk?"

Angelica could feel her eyebrows going up, and she leaned toward him curiously. Just what was the state of affairs between those two? "Do you have the ability to 'get Leah' now?"

He narrowed his eyes. "In a professional sense, yes. In a personal sense, that's none of your damn business."

"She'll tell me."

"That's her choice, not mine. And this is about you, not me. But nice try." He pointed a finger toward her head. "You still have grout in your hair." With that volley, he left the room, dodging the stain sample she threw halfheartedly after him.

She sank down against the wall, sitting on the freshly patched section of wood.

Noah wanted a relationship. But did *she* want one? Her last few forays into the dating game hadn't been spectacular. One promotional relationship with a co-star that had continued into a halfhearted fling; a three-month stint with a producer friend of Jai's; a couple of weeks with a corporate lawyer. None of them had made her feel the way Noah did.

Each of those men and her time with them had been uncomplicated … and uninspiring. Sure, they didn't often behave like Dr. Jekyll and Mister Hyde, nor did they have muddied familial relationships she hadn't known about. And there definitely hadn't been shouting matches during inexplicable arguments. But there also hadn't been days spent exploring ewok forests, or quiet conversations over great food with laughter. And the sex? Well, there was no ignoring that sex with Noah was simply the best she'd ever had.

But a relationship? She'd already broken her own

rules by sleeping with him, her business partner. She'd practically fucked him on top of their signed contract for the vineyard deal.

She nibbled on the skin around her thumbnail, worrying it between her teeth, while she considered her options.

"Angelica?" Leah's voice came from the hall.

"In here."

The makeup artist popped her head into the room. "Want to tell me what's up?"

"Only if you go first."

Leah shrugged, set her bag down inside the door, and joined Angelica on the floor. "I'm an open book, honey."

"Are you and Roger back together?"

"We're sleeping together, if that's what you're asking."

"Not exactly."

"You're asking if we're in loooooove?" Leah drawled the word with a bit of extra Southern flair in her accent, and Angelica snorted a laugh. "Who knows?"

"Would you say you're in a relationship with him?"

"Why the sudden interest in relationships?" Leah nudged her shoulder softly.

"Why are you answering my question with another question?"

"Why are you?" Leah countered with a chuckle.

"Fair enough."

"So, what's really going on?"

Angelica slid her fingers through her hair, selecting

a particularly grimy hank, and began sorting grit out of it, strand by strand. "Noah wants a relationship."

"Stubble McVineyard wants a commitment?" Leah's perfectly formed eyebrows rose as high as they could go.

Angelica nodded. "We had sex in an elevator. And then he said he wants more."

"More than elevator sex?" Leah blew out an exaggerated puff of air. "Must have been something."

"Oh, it was."

"Do *you* want more?"

"I don't know. I think I do, but then I realize I barely know the guy." She twisted her body to face Leah, not caring about the dust and grime that would lodge its way into the fibers of her jeans. "Did you know his father is some incredibly famous winemaker? And his mother is like the queen of high society, or something."

"Noah? But he wears flannel shirts and jeans with holes in the knees."

"I know." Angelica shook her head. "He also wears three-thousand-dollar suits."

Jai had given his estimate of Noah's tailoring costs before they'd parted ways for the evening. With a couple of digs about rich lumberjacks thrown in for good measure, of course.

Leah stared at Angelica for a few moments, her face morphing from thoughtful to skeptical and then determined before she settled on sympathetic. "Unless he's done something terrible you haven't mentioned, I'm failing to see the problem here. He's handsome as sin, fucks in elevators, and he's rich. Plus, he lives right next door. What's not to like?"

"I just … didn't expect him to want more." Angelica frowned. "I can handle friends with benefits. I'm *good* at friends with benefits. A relationship is …" She trailed off, uncertain.

"Honey. A relationship is what you deserve." Leah put her hand on Angelica's wrist. "He's a good guy, and he's into you. Give yourself a shot."

"You think so?"

"I do. I also think you should let me do something about your hair."

Angelica laughed. "Now that, I won't argue."

Angelica met Noah for lunch the next day. Feeling absurdly nervous, she tugged the hem of her shirt down as she sat in the window table at Frankie's and waited for him. She'd worn a cream-colored cable-knit sweater tee with a mock turtle-neck over jeans, a nod to the incoming autumn weather. The knit pattern did nice things for her curves, and she knew for certain the color was the perfect accent against the tan she'd gotten over the last few months.

A real tan! She hadn't had one of those since she'd left home at eighteen to start modeling. She admired the skin on her forearm briefly, a smattering of light freckles dotting the spot just inside her elbow, then looked up when she heard the door open.

Noah made his way straight toward her without even nodding to acknowledge the hostess. Everybody knew him, of course, so the woman just rolled her eyes and turned to greet the next customer.

"Hi," she said, smiling up at him. She'd called him after Leah had left and asked to meet. He'd suggested lunch without pressing her about what she wanted to discuss. Just as well, since she wasn't entirely sure herself.

"Hey." He pulled out the chair opposite and sat down, his eyes roaming over her like she was a glass of water in the middle of the desert.

"I asked you to give me time," she blurted without preamble.

"Yeah." He eyed her over the rim of his glass, his expression unreadable.

"I think I'm ready."

He set the drink down and leaned toward her, his gaze warm. "Ready for what?"

"For—" She was interrupted by somebody banging on the window, causing her to leap nearly out of her seat. "What the hell?" She turned and found the beaming face of one of the producers from RenoTV staring at her from underneath the painted 'F' in "Frankie's." The skinny guy with hipster glasses and a too-long tie held up a finger and mouthed "hang on."

She exchanged confused glances with Noah as the producer made a mad dash for the door.

"What's that about?" Noah muttered.

"No clue." Angelica frowned. "I don't have any meetings scheduled."

"Hi!" The man reached their table and extended a hand to Noah. "I'm so glad to meet you. And *so* glad to find you both in one place!" He shot a rapid glance at Angelica, but then his eyes quickly bounced back to Noah.

"Excuse me, but we're—" Angelica stretched her hand out to halt his verbal onslaught, but the jerk just ignored her.

"I'm Ethan Lee. One of the associate producers on Miss Travis's show." He pumped Noah's hand enthusiastically. "You're Noah Bradstone, right?"

Angelica's stomach sank as Noah's eyebrows snapped down. *Shit. That's not good*, she thought when he cast her a suspicious glare.

"I am," Noah said.

Oblivious to the lack of encouragement in Noah's tone, Ethan went back to babbling out his reason for interrupting their lunch. "It's so great that I caught you both! I was going to try to set up a meeting, but maybe we can just talk about this now to get things moving quickly?"

"Get things moving?" Noah looked over at Angelica, who did her best to project that she had no idea what was happening.

"Yes! We have a proposition for you. For both of you," Ethan corrected himself, finally turning so that Angelica was included in the conversation. Kind of him, since it was clear they were going to talk about her damn show.

"What kind of proposition?" she asked, eyes narrowed to slits. She was almost positive she wasn't going to like what he had to say.

"Well, since we found out who your famous neighbor is," Ethan nodded meaningfully at Angelica, and she felt her entire body turn cold as Noah shot a suddenly blank expression her way.

What was *that* all about? Did he honestly think she'd called the network and told them she'd found a hidden pocket of high society in River Hill? She hadn't even known about his other life until the night of the gala. But she didn't have time to think about any of this, because Ethan was prattling on.

"We've had the whole marketing team working on how we might be able to expand on the foundation you've built here."

"What do you mean?" Somehow, she got the words out while Noah's eyes bored into her from across the table.

"Well, we'd really like to include some shots of Mr. Bradstone here to show how you're marketing to the higher end of society, you know? A full feature role, honestly." Ethan turned back to Noah with an encouraging nod. "And no need to worry—the network is happy to provide wardrobe and makeup. Even some extras in your tasting room for parties, if you'd like. Get a real vibe going there, you know?"

Noah's expression transformed from blank to

frozen, and Angelica grimaced. "Um, can you give us some time to talk about it?" she asked.

"Oh, sure." Ethan bobbed his head again, like some kind of puppet. "Just let me know when you're ready to get it all in writing!" He shook Angelica's hand, not seeming to notice that Noah hadn't extended his own. "My number is on your call sheet, Miss Travis," he informed her, beaming at both of them before making his way out of Frankie's.

"That was … unexpected," she mused, hoping Noah didn't think Ethan's proposal had been her idea. Who on earth had put that bug in RenoTV's ear?

"Was it?"

"Um, yes." She frowned. "I'm just as confused as you are."

"I highly doubt that," he answered, crossing his arms and staring out the window.

"Don't be like that," she said, anger spiking through her. Why did he always assume the worst of her?

"Like what?"

"Like you think I'm some sort of monster whose only goal in life is to impinge on your idyllic life here in quaint little River Hill." She was being cruel, she knew, but so was he. How dare he act as though she were some sort of cackling villainess every time one tiny thing didn't go his way?

He snorted in response, and she took a deep breath to calm her exasperated nerves. They weren't going to get anywhere sniping at each other.

She tried to remind herself that she'd asked him

here so they could discuss how a relationship might work between them. She didn't know if that was a good idea, but she had feelings for him that she wanted to explore.

"Talk to me," she said, trying not to make it sound like a plea. "Tell me what you're thinking." She could probably guess, based on the fact that his hand was fisted around his napkin in a grip tight enough to turn his knuckles white.

"I think you have a lot of fucking nerve."

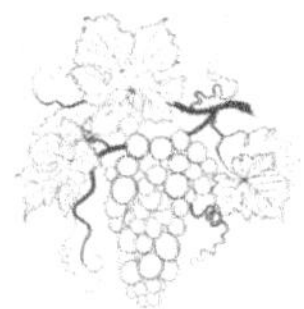

CHAPTER SEVENTEEN

"Excuse me?" Angelica stammered. "I don't think—"

"Oh, I think you thought long and hard how best to use me," Noah said, interrupting Angelica before she could offer an excuse, but there were no excuses he hadn't heard before.

When Angelica's jaw fell open and she stared at him mutely, he shook his head sadly. He really should have known better. Hell, he *had* known better. Unfortunately, he'd let his friends convince him not to trust his instincts. That was the last time he let that happen.

"I have to admit; you had me fooled."

"Me?" she cried, her eyes darting back and forth to make sure no one was eavesdropping. Leaning close, she whispered, "I'm not the one who turned into a raging asshole overnight."

Too late, Noah realized that despite her lowered voice, the older couple to their right was eyeballing them excitedly, happy to be the first to land the latest bit of town gossip. That was probably the only thing Noah didn't like about living in a small, tight-knit community; everyone knew everyone else's business just as soon as it happened. No doubt this conversation would be common knowledge by dinnertime.

He leaned forward too, and rested his forearms on the table, his fists clenched tight in front of him. "How long did it take you to run back to your producers and tell them who I am? Did you all get a good laugh over how gullible I've been?"

"Gullible?" Angelica asked, her brows angling into a deep vee. "You are many things, Noah, but gullible is *not* one of them."

"No? I fell for your act easy enough, didn't I?"

Angelica's eyes flicked between his, searching for something. And then, with a resigned sigh, she leaned back in the booth, her expression weary and taut with hurt. "Okay, I'll play. What act is that?"

Noah jutted his chin forward. "This one right here. The doe-eyed innocent." His eyes raked over her, lingering on her pillow soft lips and all of her pretty, pretty curves. "When we both know you're actually a manipulative little vixen."

Angelica crossed her arms angrily, plumping her breasts up like an offering at the altar of all things womanly and divine.

Damn, I'm really going to miss those, he thought, dragging his eyes away.

"Out of curiosity," Angelica began, "has anyone ever

told you that you're a small-minded egotistical son of a bitch? Because if that's never happened before, consider me the first."

He suppressed a grin. For as angry as he was, he enjoyed Angelica's snarky side. He'd miss that, too.

"A couple of days ago," he answered with his best approximation of a good-natured chuckle that masked his displeasure over her duplicity. "Except it was more like 'you male chauvinist piece of shit.'"

A small, unbidden smile tugged at his lips as he remembered his conversation with Naomi at the gala. But his smile dimmed when he also recalled it was *that* discussion which had made him drop his guard in the first place, the one where he'd let himself imagine what it would be like to be in a real relationship with the woman sitting across from him. The woman who'd sold him out.

"Well, that too," she replied with a pointed, definitive nod.

Noah studied her for a moment, and a feeling of resignation washed over him. "Why'd you do it, Angelica? I thought we had something good." He paused. "Or, at least, we could have."

Her bottom lip trembled, but then she took a deep breath. With a long, slow exhale, Noah watched her face morph from enraged to resentful, through somber, and into something that looked like …disappointment? "I never said a word to anyone, Noah. You can believe me or not, but I wouldn't do that to you."

Noah *wanted* to trust her. But while her words

sounded genuine enough, the slight shifting of her eyes told a different story.

"Why don't I believe you?" he asked, voice heavy with disappointment.

She chewed on her lip and let out a thin sigh. "Okay, I told *one* person," she admitted. "My friend Leah."

"Leah?"

"The woman you've seen doing my makeup."

"So, you *did* talk about me with someone affiliated with the show?"

Angelica shook her head. "It's not like that. She's my friend. She's loyal to me, not the producers."

"If you say so." He shrugged and looked out the window. He knew the best thing to do was to stand up and leave, but he stayed glued to his seat. He couldn't bring himself to walk away from her. Not yet.

Angelica sat forward and reached out to take his hand, but he pulled it away at the last second. If she touched him, he didn't know if he could keep a level head.

Slowly, she slid her hand back and linked her fingers in front of her. "The truth is, I was struggling with everything that happened between us last weekend, and I needed someone to talk to. But I swear, Noah, she wouldn't have breathed a word."

"But someone did. If it wasn't you or Leah, who?"

"How well known is your father in this town?"

"I'm sorry?" he asked, not following her sudden change of topic.

"Your dad, the wine king or whatever he is. How

many people in River Hill know who he is? Or better yet, who you are to him?"

Noah scratched his chin. He'd skipped his morning shave, hopeful their conversation would lead to his bedroom. Angelica enjoyed the feel of his rough stubble between her thighs, and he liked seeing her all marked up. Now he wished he hadn't. "I don't hide who I am, if that's what you're getting at."

She sat up straighter in the booth. "Right. So that means *anyone* could have planted the idea to leverage your name and stature in the community in the producer's head. Literally anybody could have Googled you." Her shoulders slumped forward. "And yet, your first instinct was to blame me."

"It's the timing, Angelica," he breathed. "Nothing for months, and then bam. Suddenly Howdy Doody is in here practically salivating over the idea of introducing me as a 'character.'" He used his fingers to make air quotes.

Angelica looked away. "I swear to you, it might look that way, but it isn't."

"Tell me something," he said, and her eyes darted back to his.

"Anything."

"If you were in my shoes, how would you feel? What would your first thought have been?"

Her head bowed forward, and she fidgeted with her napkin. When she raised her face back up to his, her eyes shimmered with unshed tears. "I would have trusted you. I would have believed you."

"Why?" he asked, genuinely curious.

All evidence pointed to Angelica being the leak—or if not her directly, then her friend Leah. But what Noah saw written on her face went so far against that being the case he didn't know what to believe anymore. Was she the problem here? Or was it him?

"I would have trusted you," she sniffed, "because I care about you. Because I know you're a man of your word. Because I knew you cared about me, too." She looked away then, and a single tear slid down her cheek. "Except maybe that's not true at all."

Noah groaned and fidgeted in his seat. He *did* care about her, which was why he was so torn up over everything that had just happened. If he didn't care, he would have walked out of the restaurant without a backward glance. But because of how badly he wanted to build a future with Angelica, he'd needed to know why she'd betrayed him. Now, after hearing her impassioned plea, he found himself questioning everything.

If only the timing hadn't been so suspect, he thought, *this wouldn't be happening.*

But this wasn't the right place to be have this conversation. "Can we get out of here?" he asked, his voice cracking. He cleared his throat and tried again. "Go somewhere we can talk about this with fewer prying eyes?" It seemed like half of the restaurant was leaning in their direction.

Angelica nodded and looked around. The couple next to them who'd been eavesdropping so obviously had paid their bill and were now sitting there openly staring. "Yeah, I think that's best."

Noah reached into his wallet and threw down two twenties. He hadn't ordered anything, but they'd monopolized a table for almost an hour when there'd been a line of people waiting to be seated. Frankie's was popular for good reason.

He shrugged on his coat and caught Max's raised eyebrow from across the room. With a slight shake of his head he knew his friend would understand, he turned toward the door and settled his palm against the small of Angelica's back to guide her out of the restaurant.

When she stiffened her posture and looked over her shoulder , he dropped it. Her meaning was clear: *you do not get to touch me right now. Not after the things you accused me of.* Honestly, he couldn't blame her.

When they stepped outside, an early autumn breeze ruffled Angelica's blonde locks. He was so used to seeing her with her hair in a ponytail or a braid that when she wore it loose and wavy like this, he itched to run his fingers through it. When a lank of it whipped in front of her face and got stuck in her lip gloss, he gave in and reached up to push it behind her ear. Trailing his fingers over the silky strands as he came away, he whispered, "I love your hair."

"Noah, please," she moaned, swaying in to him. "You can't do this to me."

"Do what?" he asked, rubbing the blonde tresses between his work-roughened fingers.

"You're sending me mixed signals," she answered, her voice laced with confusion and sorrow. "You're … you're …" She let out a long huff and stepped out of reach. "You're *hurting* me," she finally finished.

Noah dropped his chin to his chest and let out a long sigh of his own. "I'm sorry." He raised his face to meet her bewildered expression. "I'm just …" He looked out over the street toward the horizon, where the sun was beginning to set into vivid oranges and purples over the mountain. "I think I need some time."

Angelica laughed, but there was no joy in the sound. "Time for what?"

Noah dragged his gaze back to hers. "Time to get my head on straight. To figure out why I keep jumping to the worst conclusions where you're concerned. Time to figure out if I can be the man you need me to be."

Angelica's jaw dropped open, and she stared at him without speaking for a moment. "Wow," she said finally. "That wasn't what I expected you to say."

"What *did* you expect?"

She shook her head slowly and chewed on her lip. "I think I expected you to tell me you couldn't do this, that even though I was telling the truth, you couldn't trust me. Honestly, I'm not sure I *can* trust you."

Noah's heart kicked in his chest. He'd had every intention of saying those same words, but now that they'd slipped from her lips instead, they lodged deep in his gut and ate a hole through his stomach lining.

As they'd exited Frankie's, he'd had an epiphany.

Clearly, he had some deep-seated issues he needed to work through. But he'd hoped they could work through them together. Now he wasn't so sure. Her saying she couldn't trust him like like a punch to the gut. Suddenly, he knew exactly how his behavior had felt to her.

How had he fucked up so badly?

Noah laced his hands behind his head and paced a circle, eventually stopping where he'd begun. "I know. Please, just think about it, though. When I'm not being a complete asshole, think about what we have. How good it is between us. What we *could* have, if I can get my shit together."

She peered at him through moistened lashes. "And what does that look like—you getting your shit together?"

He glanced away. "I don't know," he admitted, already feeling defeated. "Talk to someone, I guess. Figure out why I'm like this; why I have trust issues."

Angelica took a step forward and laid a hand on his arm. "You'd do that?"

He looked down at where her small fingers rested against the bulk of his arm, then back up to her exquisite face. "Yeah," he nodded. "I care about you, Angelica. Please don't doubt that." He'd never considered talking to somebody about the complicated ways that love, family, and trust twisted themselves around inside him.

But for Angelica—for a future with her? He'd find a way through the maze.

Eyes that were equal parts hope and caution flicked between his for a few protracted moments. In reality, only two or three seconds had passed, but it felt like the world had quit spinning and time had stood still while he waited for her response.

Eventually, she licked her lips and slid her hand from his arm. "Okay." And then she took a step back, and then another, until there might as well have been a canyon between them. "You figure out your shit, and we'll see where we stand then."

After the way he'd treated her, Noah knew that was all he could ask from her. And yet the possibility that it might already be too late for them rested heavy on his shoulders.

Still, it's a chance, he thought as he shoved his hands in his pockets and watched her rush to her car.

CHAPTER EIGHTEEN

She was giving Noah *time*, Angelica reminded herself after the third time she'd seen him exiting the coffee shop as she entered. They'd exchanged quick smiles, warm hellos, the sort of thing casual friends did. Friends who didn't have emotional conversations that felt like ripping off a decades-old Band-Aid. Friends who hadn't given each other the most incredible orgasms of their lives in varied exotic locations. Friends who just… said hi when they passed each other.

She hated it.

She wanted him back.

For all her brave words after he'd run roughshod over her about not being able to trust him, she was veering dangerously close to begging him to come back to her, no matter what.

And that was a major red flag for her.

Noah wasn't the only one with some things to work out it seemed.

If he was going to get his shit together, she owed him the courtesy of doing the same by figuring out what she wanted before she threw herself at him. If he wanted a relationship when he was done taking time, she needed to be sure she still wanted one, too.

Sex wasn't everything, no matter how much she missed it.

She took a break from filming for a few days; they were at a standstill waiting for backordered tile for the kitchen anyway, so she left Roger and the crew to film shots of River Hill and the Harvest Festival preparations and flew home to see her parents for the weekend.

Her mother greeted her with open arms and a paint-covered smock; her father promptly confiscated her laptop to install a new software system on it. Her family enveloped her in its warm, slightly stifling embrace, and she resolved to forget about Noah for at least forty-eight hours.

It didn't work, of course.

Her mother had spoken to Jai recently, and now she wanted to hear all about the gala. And there was no fooling Elaine Travis when it came to leaving important details out. There was a Noah-shaped hole in Angelica's careful narrative, and her mother sniffed right through the descriptions of dresses and food to find it.

"And was anyone else there? Someone special?" Her

mother handed her a cracker loaded with a slice of sharp cheddar cheese imported from upstate New York. "Try this one. The farm they make it on is the cutest thing you've ever seen."

"Farms aren't cute, Mom. They smell like cows."

"Cute cows. Eat your cheese and tell your mother the truth."

Angelica sighed. "You remember my neighbor, Noah?" She'd kept her parents apprised of the situation, especially the part where he was growing vines on her property, but she'd left out the sex. Her mother had probably figured it out, though.

"The wine guy, right?"

Angelica nodded and reached out for another slice of cheese. It really *was* good, though she wouldn't vouch for the cuteness of the cows it had come from. "Turns out he's a big deal."

"Everyone in California is a big deal," her mother said with a smile. "Even you."

"A different kind of big deal," she explained with a smile in return for her mother's loyalty. Her parents had hosted screenings of every single one of her movies. "It turns out his father is some kind of wine baron."

"Like a Rockefeller, but with grapes?" Her mother pursed her lips in thought. "Intriguing."

"Yes, and he's … got some issues."

"The father or the son?"

"The son because of the father, I think." Angelica snagged a grape from the tray on the counter. "He's really touchy about people trying to take advantage of him based on his family name."

Elaine Travis looked at her daughter sternly. "Did you?"

"No. At least, not on purpose."

"Well, that sounds like two different answers." She touched Angelica's nose with one extended finger. "What's the truth?"

"The producers found out about him, probably just by Googling, I would imagine." She was positive Leah hadn't said anything. Jai might have, but really, the RenoTV people were all in on showcasing River Hill's charm, so presumably they'd done their research. Anybody could use a search engine, and Noah wasn't really hiding his last name. "And they jumped all over him to try to lend his name to the show."

"What did you say?"

Angelica felt a familiar sourness in the pit of her stomach. "Not enough, I think."

"What happened?"

"We had a fight. He doesn't trust me."

"Is that the end of it?"

"Well, no." She could feel herself heating with a blush, for some reason. "He knows he's got some stuff to work on, so he's talking to somebody about it."

"And what are you doing?"

"Eating cheese with my mother."

Her mother frowned. "What do you want, Angelica? Should I be the supportive mother and say he did you wrong, and that he's no good? Or is this a situation where you need to figure out how you can be a part of this relationship without giving up your right to be a trustworthy person?" She leaned forward. "Because I know you can be trusted. But I think you need to trust *yourself* to make the right decisions."

"I was ready to say yes to it all," Angelica confessed. "Commitment, dating, real relationship stuff. And then he blew up at me and I freaked out."

"But he's working on it, yes?"

"Yeah."

"So, is he worth it?"

Angelica blew out a breath. "God, yes."

"Then stand up for yourself and get the relationship you want and need," her mother said firmly. "No more running away."

"Not even for cute cheese?" Angelica held up the last slice.

"Love trumps cheese, Angelica."

S he'd had plenty of time to think on the flight back to California, but she hadn't had time at all to prepare for the sight that greeted her when she exited the airport terminal to hail a cab, her well-traveled carry-on rolling behind her. The wheels of the suitcase bumped into her heels as she stopped dead to gape at Noah leaning casually against his truck with Molly's leash wrapped around his wrist. His hand rested gently against the dog's head as she sat obediently on the curb next to him.

"What are you doing here?" Angelica blurted before the thought finished making its way through her brain.

His smile was almost shy. "Well, I heard you were coming in today, and Molly thought you might need a ride."

Angelica looked down at Molly's smiling doggy face and wagging tail and couldn't help but smile in return. "I could use one."

"Hop in." He opened the door for her, and clicked his tongue at Molly, who leapt cheerfully into her customary place in back.

"Thanks."

Angelica buckled herself in and waited until Noah pulled into less complicated traffic than the arrivals line to ask, "So, how are things going?" She couldn't bring herself to ask, "Are you better yet?" or, "How's your trust stuff coming?" Or even, "My place or yours?"

"Slowly," he said without taking his eyes off the road. "I never realized I was so complicated."

"Yes, you seem so simple, what with your flannel shirts hung next to the expensive suits and all," she said dryly.

"Hey, at least they're organized."

She laughed. "Maybe you'll even expand your wardrobe after all this."

"I'm going to a counselor, not the fashion police."

"Baby steps."

"How was your trip?" He flipped on his blinker and

merged smoothly across two lanes, hitting the exit for the state route that would take them through the valley and into River Hill.

"It was really good. My parents are great." She smiled. "In small doses, anyway."

"Your mom is an artist, right?"

She nodded. "She had me pick out the paintings I want to hang in the inn while I was there."

"What does your dad do?"

"He's an accountant." Suddenly she felt awkward. They were discussing her parents, but it was who *his* parents were that had landed them in this strange space where they were friends but not lovers … but not just friends either. Maybe avoiding talking about family was best.

"Did I miss anything in River Hill?" she asked, switching topics.

"Sean won a drinking contest."

"Is that … good?" She frowned. She'd met Sean's mother and she didn't think the nice lady who'd come to her house as part of the town council's proposal would be thrilled about her son's excessive drinking.

"Not really. He's got some stuff of his own going on." Noah's tone turned thoughtful. "Maybe I'll bring him my counselor's card."

"If he's ready for it." Angelica sighed. "Different people cope in different ways."

"Well, drinking himself into the next day isn't really coping."

"True."

"What else …" Noah mused, moving on from the topic of his friend's fragile emotional state. "Max is considering taking the tacos off the menu for the season."

"No!" Angelica gasped. "He can't!"

"So you'll sign my petition, then?"

"Damn right I will. Good lord, I was only gone for the weekend and he goes and does something like that?"

"Guess you'll have to stick around." Noah turned his head away from the road to grin at her briefly, and she smiled back until the moment turned thick and strange.

Angelica swallowed around a golf-ball sized lump in her throat. This was *hard*. Was he ready?

Come to think of it, was *she* ready?

Talking with her parents had clarified a few things, but there was still a part of her that wondered if Noah could really find his way past whatever had made him continuously blow up at her. His comment about things going slowly made it seem like that time hadn't yet come, and she resigned herself to small talk for the rest of the ride.

Noah left her at her doorstep with a wave and a wag of the tail from Molly, and she carried her bag inside, promptly tripping over boxes of tile somebody had left just inside the door. "Dammit!"

"Angelica?" It was Leah's voice, coming from upstairs.

"I'm here."

"Hey." Leah's voice sounded strange, Angelica realized. It was oddly thick, as though she'd been … crying? *What the hell?* Leah never cried.

Angelica hauled ass upstairs and slammed her way into the first of the guest rooms. "What's wrong?"

Leah was huddled in the middle of a new bed that had been delivered the week before, surrounded by packages of linens Angelica hadn't yet unfolded and set out. Her friend's knees were drawn up to her chest and her wrists were crossed in front of her ankles, her forehead cradled in the space between her denim-clad kneecaps. Something must really be wrong if Leah was wearing jeans. Angelica hadn't realized she owned any.

"Leah." She crossed to the bed and sat down next to the tiny ball of woman Leah had contorted herself into. "What's going on?"

Leah sniffed. "Roger asked me to marry him."

Well, *that* wasn't what she'd expected to hear. Angelica opened her mouth, then closed it again, then very carefully asked, "Is that good or bad?"

"Both." Leah's voice was muffled, since her face was pressed against her knees.

"Hey." Angelica reached over and pried her friend's head up. "Talk to me."

Leah's eyes were puffy, but her makeup was still perfect—waterproofing was a miraculous invention. She rubbed her nose with the back of her hand and sighed. "I thought it was just for fun. We were sleeping together, having some good times."

"So, you don't want to marry him?"

"I don't know." She sighed. "It's gotten … intense lately. I'm not used to being the first thing somebody thinks about when they wake up."

"Is *he* the first thing you think about when you wake up?"

"I mean, like, eighty percent of the time, yeah. Sometimes I wake up thinking about breakfast, you know?"

"Do you love him?"

"I've loved him for years, Angelica. That doesn't mean I should marry him."

"What do you mean?"

Leah flopped backwards on the bed, her head resting on a plastic-wrapped pillow. "Love that doesn't go anywhere is a pretty safe kind of love," she answered thoughtfully.

"Like unrequited love?"

"As long as we weren't together, I could say he was the one that got away and go about my merry little way."

"And now that you're together again?"

"Well, he doesn't want to get away. And I don't think I do either."

"But?"

"Marriage is a big fucking deal, Angelica." Leah bolted upright. "Look at you. You were a mess when Noah asked you just to *date* him."

She held up her hands. "Don't make this about me! I have my own issues. We're talking about yours right now." She ignored the little flash of wistful imagination that sent a mental picture of herself in a gauzy white gown, standing with Noah under the blooming wisteria in the backyard of her inn under a warm California sunset.

"Do you think you're ready to get married?" Angelica asked, pushing that fanciful notion deep down into the black pit of her soul where it wouldn't bother her again.

"I have no idea."

"Do you want to find out?" she pressed.

Leah was silent for a long time, but then said, "Maybe."

"What are you going to say to Roger?"

"I don't know."

Angelica leaned forward to hug her friend. "Well, if you say yes, I want to be a bridesmaid. And if you say no, I'll take you out drinking and we'll buy a fancy dress anyway. How's that?"

Leah hugged her back, resting her forehead on Angelica's shoulder. "Bases covered. You're a good friend."

"So are you," Angelica said. "The best."

When Noah called to ask her to dinner a week later, she could tell by his tone he'd come to some kind of decision.

They'd run into each other a few more times during the week, but the vaguely friendly exchanges they'd been having before he'd picked her up at the airport had transformed into something warmer and more anticipatory, though they hadn't really said more than a few words.

And by god, she missed touching him.

They'd settled on an early dinner at Frankie's—where else?—and she dressed with care, aware of every caress of the silk blouse over her skin as she slid it on. She paired it with tight, dark-washed jeans—not the boot-cut ones she wore on a daily basis, most of which were now firmly cemented with various home repair products. No, these jeans were the ones she saved for occasions when she wanted her curves to do the talking. If Noah had come to the right decision, he'd be rewarded. If he hadn't, well, he'd know what he was missing out on, that was for sure.

She slid into the booth opposite him and smiled as he handed her a glass already filled with wine. "Yours?"

"Special bottling, just for Frankie's," he said with a matching smile. He'd chosen a booth along the side wall this time, not the window table and not the quiet, private corner booth. She tried not to overthink what that might mean.

"Thanks," she said, taking a sip. The wine rolled down her throat, crisp and clean.

"You look great," he said.

"Thanks," she said again, then pursed her lips as she realized she was mindlessly repeating the same word over and over. "What are you having?"

"Carnitas, I think." He nodded thoughtfully. "You?"

"That sounds good, actually. If I can't have the tacos. When's that petition going through?"

"I need like three more signatures before there are so many that the state legislature is legally obligated to address it."

"Nice." She laughed.

They managed to place their orders, drink more wine, and get through dinner with small talk before Angelica got up the nerve to bring up what they were here for.

She set her fork down after one last bite of tender pork, the clink of it hitting the plate seeming to echo through the entire room. "So, what did you really want to talk about?"

There was a pause as he sipped his wine again. Then he said it. The word she'd been waiting for.

"Us."

She sat back in her seat, exhaling. "All right. Let's talk about us."

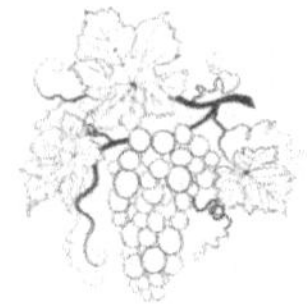

CHAPTER NINETEEN

*U*s. There, he'd said it.

But that was only the first step in making Angelica his.

He knew he had a lot to make up for, but he would gladly spend the rest of his life trying if she'd let him. Now, he just needed to convince her that he was worth the risk.

"First," he said, setting his glass to the side, "I owe you a massive apology." Angelica opened her mouth to interrupt him, but he shook his head. "Please, let me finish."

When she gritted her teeth and sat back in the booth, Noah reached across the table and set his hand atop hers. Squeezing it gently, he continued, "I haven't always been fair to you. I know now that it had nothing to do with who *you* are, and everything to do with who *I* am. Who I'd become without even realizing it."

"What do you mean?" she asked, pushing her plate aside and smiling at the bus boy who'd stopped by to clear their table.

Noah dragged his eyes away and stared out over the busy restaurant for a few moments. Dimly, he was aware of the sound of Max's laughter, the clinking of glasses, and the chatter of happy patrons, but all he really could hear was the sound of his own heart beating a whir in his head. *Thump, thump, thump.*

While it had been difficult to discuss all of this with his therapist, doing so with the woman he loved and wanted to spend the rest of his life with was even harder. Especially since the things he'd discovered about himself, and the reasons why he'd been so awful to Angelica in the first place, weren't exactly points in his favor.

Still, all he could do was be honest and hope for the best.

But before he could answer, their waiter approached. "Would you care for dessert this evening? It's not on the menu, but we've got a triple chocolate brownie for two, paired with a coffee ice cream made with espresso from The Hollow Bean." Max was nothing if not encouragingly unsubtle.

Noah raised his eyebrows to Angelica, who patted her stomach. "Sorry, none for me. Max outdid himself with those carnitas."

"None for me, thanks. Just the check when you get a chance."

The waiter pulled a small folio from his apron and set it on the table, letting them know he'd be back shortly.

Noah placed enough cash inside to cover the bill and a generous tip for the staff, and then canted his head toward the door. "It's a beautiful night. Want to take a walk around the square with me?"

Angelica slid across the leather banquette and shrugged into her jacket. When she'd finished wrapping the paisley scarf around her neck, he set his hand on the small of her back and led her from the restaurant, waving to Max as they went.

As they strolled down the sidewalk hand-in-hand, the storefronts lining the square glowing from within, they made more small talk.

Noah described an interview he'd done for a profile on winemakers under forty, while Angelica brought him up to speed on the latest with the inn's renovations. When they reached the end of the square, he pulled her into the park, toward the gazebo. The delicate structure had been decorated with gourds in every shape, size, and color in anticipation of the coming Harvest Fair.

They took a seat on one of the iron benches that wrapped its edges, and Noah wrapped an arm around her shoulder, savoring the feel of her against him.

There'd been a few dark moments when he thought he might never get to touch her again. Might never *deserve* to touch her again. His heart kicked in his chest, and his belly churned with uncertainty. He'd unraveled so much in such a short time, but he still sometimes felt as though he might tangle it all up again.

Especially when he was trying to prove himself to her.

Almost as if Angelica could sense his anxiety, she scooted out from his embrace and said, "Not that I'm not enjoying this, but you mentioned something about a realization you'd had?"

He twisted on the bench and rested his arm on its back. "I've always considered myself a feminist. I'm a hard advocate for equal pay for everyone I employ. I participate in the March for Women every year, and I pay attention to the issues surrounding women's rights. I *know* I do." He cleared his throat uncomfortably. Saying *that* had been easy; *this* was the harder part. "The problem is, I … uh … apparently harbor some antiquated notions of what I'm looking for in a relationship."

"I'm not sure I'm following," Angelica said, her head tilting to the side as she studied him, her eyes reflecting the glittering white fairy lights that had just flashed on in the square.

I could get lost in those eyes, Noah thought briefly before he continued explaining himself. "You met my mother. I'm sure you didn't miss the fact that she's not the warmest person in the room."

Angelica opened her mouth to speak, but then closed it and shook her head. "Nope, not going there."

He chuckled. "I love my mom, really. But I *always* wanted her to be a different type of mother. The one who would kiss my knee when I fell down, or who would bring sliced oranges to my baseball games."

"Sounds like my mom. Of course, she also got thrown out of a few of my games for yelling at the ref. You take the good with the bad, I suppose." Her luscious mouth split into an impish grin.

Unable to return it, Noah dropped his eyes and stared at the black veining in the marble floor. "My mom never went to my games, no matter how many times I asked her to."

"I'm sorry," Angelica replied, her voice filled with sympathy, as she set her hand on his shoulder. "That must have been difficult for you."

He nodded once, briskly. And then he pulled a deep breath into his lungs. *Better to get this over with*, he thought. "The thing is—and I know it's old fashioned and backward—but I need to know the woman I'm with will *always* put our kids first."

Angelica's brows furrowed deeply. She pulled her hand away and leaned back, putting a few extra inches between them. "And you don't think I'm that sort of woman."

It wasn't a question so much as a statement of fact.

Which was why Noah owed her an apology and explanation. "It's not that. I actually think you'd be a great mom," he said, raising his eyes to hers.

The problem was, he wanted her to be *his* kids' mom, but he was afraid their timing was all off. That no matter how much he might love her, their lives weren't compatible.

"I hear a 'but' in there somewhere."

Noah scanned the square briefly and then dragged his eyes back to Angelica. "I'm making a mess of this."

She sat up, her back ramrod straight, and folded her hands in her lap. "I have to admit, this isn't how I envisioned this conversation going."

"I know," he sighed, and reached for her hand. At first, she resisted, but eventually gave in. He rubbed his thumb in circles over her palm. "I asked you for time to figure out my shit, and even though I've been a complete asshole, you gave it to me. What I want to say is that I want it all with you—the big house, the dog, the kids, and I want it sooner rather than later."

Angelica sucked in a startled gasp and her eyes flew to his. Flicking between them, she whispered, "What do you mean?"

He wrapped his arm around her shoulder and pulled her flush against his side. "I've never felt about anyone the way I feel about you, Angelica. But I'm almost thirty-five, and I want to start a family. I want so much for those kids to be yours, but—"

Angelica pushed against his chest and leaned back, their eyes locking. She licked her lips. "Did you just say you want to marry me?" she croaked.

Noah's lips hitched up. "Don't worry," he chuckled nervously. "I don't mean tomorrow. But yes, eventually. Sooner, rather than later preferably. But—"

"There you are!" Ethan Lee interrupted, rushing

into the gazebo and sliding to a stop in front of them. His cheeks were flushed, his coat was buttoned incorrectly, and his hair stuck up in several different directions.

Noah had heard the footsteps thundering along the grass, but he'd been so wrapped up in Angelica he hadn't looked up, assuming it was a jogger. Instead, it was his least favorite person in River Hill.

Ethan beamed his goofy smile directly at Angelica. "I've been looking everywhere for you. You're never going to believe the offer I have from RenoTV!"

"Hey, Ethan." Angelica scooted further away from Noah and smoothed her long blonde locks into a thick waterfall over her left shoulder. Noah watched her take a deep breath before she asked, "What's up?" Her tone wasn't exactly friendly, but she wasn't using words like 'buzz off' or 'not now, dammit,' either.

Damn. He'd screwed it up again. Hadn't been able to muddle through his explanations well enough, hadn't explained that he wanted her happiness above everything. Fuck, he hadn't even managed to tell her that he loved her.

Call it a premonition, but the physical space she'd put between them felt like the beginning of their end. He'd said he wanted them to build a life together, and instead of telling Ethan to give them a minute, she'd turned her attention from Noah to discuss work.

Stupid fucking Ethan. Noah shoved his hands into his coat pocket. *Always ruining everything.*

Indifferent to the tense mood radiating in waves off the gazebo's other inhabitants, Ethan forged on. "I just got off the phone with the bigwigs over there, and they *loved* the early footage we sent them. Salivating. They said you're a natural."

Angelica smiled thinly. "That's terrific."

He nodded, his big head bobbing with excitement on his pencil-thin neck. "It is! But that's not all."

Noah's heart sank. He didn't know how he knew it, but he was certain the next words out of Howdy Doody's mouth would change everything.

"They want to give us a whole series!" Ethan bellowed, his eyes flashing with victory. "They're ready to sign you to a three-year deal *today*. They want to set you up with a different project in a different location each season. Season one will obviously be the inn here in River Hill, and I was thinking next season we can go to—"

"That's great, Ethan," Angelica interrupted, rising from the bench to stop the flow of words and brushing her hands down the front of her jeans. "The thing is, I'm kind of in the middle of something here, so ...."

She glanced toward Noah, her eyes filled with contrition ... and something else he couldn't quite identify. Then, looking back to her producer, she continued, "Can you send me the details over email so I can go through them tonight, and we can talk about it tomorrow?"

"Um, sure." His eyes flew to Noah's, hard and glinting, before his face resumed its normal, good-natured countenance. Blowing into his hands to warm them, he said, "I have to say though, I figured you would have been a bit more excited by this opportunity. Breaks like this don't come along every day."

Angelica nodded. "I am excited. Thank you for telling me. We'll chat tomorrow, okay?" She looked pointedly at him, and when it became clear she wasn't going to bend on this, Ethan sighed and tossed her a tight-lipped nod.

"Fine, tomorrow then. How about we discuss the offer over coffee at The Hollow Bean. Say 8 a.m.?"

"Make it ten and you've got yourself a date."

"Fine. Ten it is," Ethan bit out, his eyes flashing with malice before he stomped away.

Noah wasn't surprised by Ethan's reaction. The producer had tried to mask his darker side the few times their paths had crossed after that first encounter at Frankie's—and Noah's terse, emailed rejection—but in the end, he'd shown his true colors. He despised Noah for not agreeing to participate in the show or let them license his family's name, and now he blamed Noah for Angelica's restrained reaction, too.

At least their dislike was mutual.

Noah had considered telling Angelica how Ethan had gone ballistic during their one-on-one, but then things had become strained between them, and he'd decided not to interfere in her business decisions.

Now though …well, now things had changed.

He had changed.

Even if Angelica decided she didn't want to build a life with him, he cared deeply about her, and he wanted her to be aware of exactly what kind of person Ethan was so she'd understand just who she'd be partnering with if she moved forward with this new opportunity. But because of how fractious he'd been in the past where the show was concerned, he knew he'd have to tread carefully. Especially since he was trying to prove to her he was a changed man, one who didn't fly off the handle at the first sign of provocation.

"Sorry about that," she said, drawing circles in the fallen leaves with the toe of her boot. She raised her eyes to Noah. "For what it's worth, I wasn't expecting that." With wary eyes, she chewed on her lip, and her shoulders tensed, like she was just waiting for him to blow up at her any second.

His gut churned. He hated that he was the cause of that look on her face. This new opportunity was a huge break, and she should be happy they wanted to expand her show. But rather than being excited, she was worried about his reaction. So as much as he wanted Angelica to stay in River Hill with him, he put on his big boy pants and did the right thing.

"I know." Noah tugged Angelica into his embrace. With his arms wrapped around her waist and his chin resting on the top of her head, he said, "Congratulations, sweetheart. I'm proud of you." He dropped a kiss to her hair and leaned back. "You deserve every good thing that comes your way, Angelica."

She searched his face for a few brief seconds, and

then shook her head and huffed out a laugh. "I honestly don't know what to say. I thought for sure you'd be angry."

Noah led her back to their bench. "I don't love the idea of you leaving, but I … I love you … and I want you to be happy. I know this show makes you happy."

When her eyes shone with gladness, he knew he'd said the right thing—even if his chest hurt and his gut churned with acid. Thank God he'd managed to get it out. He wanted her to hear it, no matter what happened.

"Oh, Noah." Angelica launched herself into his arms and kissed him hard. She laughed a happy, tinkling sound he'd dream about for as long as he lived. He wasn't sure there was a better sound in all the world than her magical laughter. "You certainly know how to keep a girl on her toes."

His lips hitched up in a rueful grin. "I certainly try."

Angelica rested her palm on Noah's cheek, and he leaned into it. "I meant what I said to Ethan. I need to see the details before I make any decisions," she said.

He put on a brave face. *This is the right thing to do*, he reminded himself.

He loved Angelica, and that meant supporting her dreams—even if they didn't align with his own. He hadn't always understood that, but now he did. He just wished things had turned out differently.

"You should do it."

"Even if the pay is shit and they want to work me to the bone?" she joked.

Noah smiled. "No, not then."

"And ..." her eyes dropped to her lap, and her hand slid along his scruff until Noah's face was cold for the loss of her heat. "There's us to consider as well."

Us.

There it was. That word again.

"Look at me," Noah said, his voice coming out like gravel. This was possibly the hardest thing he'd ever done, but he needed to get the words out.

When she raised her eyes to his, he continued, "I love you, Angelica. And loving you means wanting you to succeed. So, if this is what you want, I'll support you. I don't know what a long-distance relationship would look like, but if you're game, I'd be willing to try."

Her dreams—her success—meant everything. He could wait awhile, if it meant she would stay with him. And if she wouldn't, he'd probably still wait.

She chewed her lip again. "You would?"

Noah nodded. "Yeah, I would."

"But what about all that other stuff you said earlier. About wanting to start a family?"

Noah lifted his shoulder in what he hoped looked like a nonchalant shrug. "Sure. I'm old, but not decrepit. As long as I can still carry you to my bed, I think I'll be okay."

Her eyes flicked between his. "We'll figure something out." It was a vague promise, and they both knew it. He'd take it anyway.

He stood and reached for her hand. "In the meantime, let's get you home. It's getting cold."

Angelica placed her hand in his, and together they walked out of the park.

When they reached her car, he pushed a lock of hair behind her ear, and his hands skated down her neck. "Can I kiss you?"

She laughed, a happy girlish sound. "If you don't, I'm going to kiss you."

He leaned forward and pressed his mouth against hers. She sighed, and he sucked her breath into his lungs, making Angelica a part of him. He parted her lips, and she let him lick his way inside, their tongues tangling in a dance as old as time. Her hands knotted in his hair, and she tugged at the roots, pulling a groan from him.

God, he missed this.

"Come home with me," he implored. "I need you."

Angelica eased away from him and smiled. "As much as I want that too, I think I should head home. I have some important things to think about, and when I see you naked, I am incapable of coherent speech, let alone logical thought. Can I get a raincheck?"

Noah swallowed. "Of course. If you change your mind, I'll leave the door unlocked."

Angelica rose up on her tiptoes and placed a quick, feather-light kiss on his lips before climbing into her car. She hesitated a moment before closing the door, but then did so with a shake of her head.

Noah stood on the curb and watched her pull out of her parking space, his hands fisted in his pockets. She turned to him and waved.

He forced a smile to his lips and waved back as he watched her drive down the road. And, he feared, straight out of his life.

CHAPTER TWENTY

Angelica shut the door of the inn behind her and leaned against it, blowing out a long breath. She felt like she'd spent the last two hours skydiving with a bungee cord attached to her middle, yanking her back and forth through the clouds in great heaving swings with yawning drops in between. It was, perhaps, an overwrought analogy, she reflected as she shoved herself upright and headed to the kitchen.

She needed coffee. And to check her email.

An hour later, she unfurled her shoulders and sat straight on the stool by the kitchen island, rubbing her temples to try and ease the ache she often got from staring at her laptop in the dark for hours on end.

Why hadn't she turned the lights on? Just because she *could* make coffee in the dark didn't mean she *should*. She glanced at her drained mug and grimaced.

What was she going to do?

Noah loved her and wanted to marry her. The

thought rolled through her entire body like a warm wave, reminding her of the brief time in her early modeling career when she'd done a couple of tropical photoshoots. She'd laid in the sand and the clear turquoise water had cascaded over her body up to her elbows while the photographers snapped away and the director yelled vaguely obscene instructions. She'd almost been able to tune him out as the ocean caressed her.

Of course, when she'd gotten up, there'd been nearly a bucketful of sand in her bikini bottom. Nothing came without a price.

And the proverbial sand in today's bikini was definitely Ethan Lee and the offer from RenoTV. Golden sand, specifically. It was a good offer. And Noah seemed like he wanted her to take it.

Well, no. He'd said he wanted her to be *happy,* and if that meant leaving, he supported her.

But would leaving make her happy?

Hell, no.

She scowled and read the email again. Her mother was right. It was time for her to stop running and start fighting for what she wanted. Time to work for the relationship and life she deserved. With that thought in mind, she picked up her phone.

Angelica: Are u there?

Her agent responded to her text immediately, as she'd expected him to. He never went to sleep before two o'clock in the morning.

Jai: What's up, buttercup?

Angelica: Did u get their email?

There was a slightly longer pause, and she watched the little dots on the screen that indicated he was typing.

Jai: Yes.

She snorted and wondered what he'd typed before deciding on that simple, one-word answer. It had taken far too long for him to have punched in three letters.

Angelica: What do u think?

Jai: I think it's up to you.

Angelica: That's not helpful.

Jai: Fine. Hold on while I re-read it.

A few minutes passed, and then those flickering dots appeared again.

Jai: Okay, terms are good, exposure is good, and the commitment is a little high, but not unusual for TV. Agent analysis complete. Now what?

She pursed her lips and turned back to the email still on her screen.

Angelica: How flexible do u think they are?

Jai: Flexible how?

Angelica: Look at the second paragraph.

Jai: Angelica Travis, are you saying what I think you're saying?

Angelica: Yes. I want to …wait for it … negotiate.

All Jai sent back were fireworks and party emojis, and she laughed before setting her phone to mute. She had somewhere to be and she didn't want interruptions.

hen Noah answered the door shirtless, wearing only a pair of lounge pants that hid nothing, Angelica grinned, feeling squirming anticipation course through her body—especially the parts that were looking forward to being in contact with his.

"Hi."

"Um, hi." He blinked and rubbed the sleep from his eyes. "I didn't expect you, to be honest."

"I know. I'm sorry, I shouldn't have been so vague earlier."

"You weren't vague," he protested. "You were right. It's an incredible offer."

"Well, it's not *bad*, but it's also not quite how our little buddy Ethan put it, either." She pushed past him into the house and tugged him toward the couch. "I have no idea why he presented it like it was all travel, all the time."

Noah muttered something that sounded suspiciously like "I bet I know."

"What?"

"Nothing."

"Not a fan of Mister Lee, are you?" she teased.

"Not really." He sat on the couch where she pointed.

"I don't blame you. His social skills need a lot of work before he gets that big promotion he's angling for." She settled down into the cushions and cuddled in next to him, enjoying the way Noah's arm immediately came around her, drawing her even closer.

"So, what's the deal?" His voice was muffled by her hair as he pressed his lips to her head, and she was distracted by his hands sliding slowly up her belly, taking her shirt with them.

"Mmm," she murmured. "What?"

He tickled her, and she let out a quiet shriek.

"Tell me what you're thinking," he said, tapping his fingers against her bare skin to emphasize his words.

She laughed and laced her fingers through his over her stomach. "They want to offer me a multi-season deal. But I think, and Jai agrees, that the seasons beyond this first one could very well be in a different format."

"Like what?"

"Much as I've loved renovating the inn, I honestly don't know if I have it in me to do it again, full-scale," she admitted.

Angelica had loved every minute of the transformation of her inn, but she'd also enjoyed being on camera again. The burnout from years of Hollywood horrors had faded when she'd surrounded herself with a good team and a project she was fully invested in. One that was about more than just a job. And the leverage that gave her, along with reviews from test audiences who'd viewed the pilot that were far more glowing than Ethan had described, was pretty significant.

"Jai and I think they might be open to me hosting the show, rather than having me in charge of every project," she explained. "Instead of moving somewhere and taking on a huge renovation myself, I could base myself here and fly out to shoot episodes of other people's renovation projects in similar small towns. Go out there for a month, shoot some footage on the town, lend a hand on the really fun parts—"

"The messy parts, you mean," he interrupted with a light pinch to her side.

She chuckled. "Apparently the more building materials you have stuck in your hair, the more TV audiences like you. Who knew?"

"You'd stay here, then?" he asked.

Angelica recognized that he'd tried to keep his voice neutral, but she hadn't missed the faint note of hope and longing his question had conveyed.

"I still want to run the inn," she said. "I might need to hire some help, but I've got a few people in mind."

Her dad wasn't too far from retirement, and he would be thrilled to start using some of the bookkeeping software he'd been researching for a real-life purpose. And her mother's art would sell like gangbusters in River Hill and the surrounding areas. The large storage shed located out back could easily convert to a studio. If Noah really was interested in a big, boisterous close-knit family, he'd definitely get one with her.

She grinned at him, letting his returning smile warm her. "Yes, I'd stay."

But before he could kiss her, she held up a hand. "But I'd travel still, you know that, right? You can't host a show without going places, sometimes for long shoots."

"Honey, as long as you come back to me, I couldn't care less." He nuzzled her neck, then stilled. "Do you think you could bring back some grapes from the East Coast? I've been thinking of trying this cloning technique I read about—"

"I don't even know where I'm going yet," she protested. "For that matter, I don't know if they'll say yes." Even though everything was still up in the air, she hadn't wanted to wait to share her plans with Noah. She wanted him involved; she wanted him invested in every facet of her life.

She wanted to be the first thing he thought about when he woke up, just like Leah had said.

"What if they say no?" he asked.

"Then I'll still have an inn to run," she shrugged.

Really, she'd loved being in front of the camera again, but if the network wasn't down with her proposal, she knew she could walk away from it. She had a lot to live for here in River Hill, after all.

"And this place could use some sprucing up," she teased. "I hear there's a closet reorganization in order."

She didn't get any more out before he wrapped his arms around her and pushed her straight back onto the couch, covering her entire body with his own. His lips were on hers, his tongue licking gently into her mouth to tangle with her own as his leg pressed between hers. When his hand slid down to tug at the waist of her pants, she wriggled underneath him to help. His swift intake of breath made her smile.

"You're on board with my plan?" she asked in between kisses.

"So *incredibly* on board, my love," he said.

And then they didn't talk at all.

"And we all know Max," Angelica said two days later, smiling into the camera as it panned back to her from the crowd cheering the handsome chef on as he set up a table of desserts for hungry Harvest Festival-goers in front of his restaurant. Roger spun his finger above the red light to indicate that she should continue speaking to draw their time out. "If you've spent any time in River Hill, you've been to Frankie's. And if you're planning a visit, I'm happy to report that the Oakwell Inn is now accepting bookings."

It was her very last interview session, and they'd moved on from discussing the specifics of her completed renovations to the town square where she was taking her viewers on a tour of the Harvest Festival, as promised. And holding a glass of Noah's best red as she did, his winery's logo etched on the bowl and clearly visible between her fingers. It was their compromise. She wanted his business to thrive on its own merits, and not his famous family name—but she was happy to lend *her* name, and her show, to every business in River Hill, Stonewell Vineyards very much included. She'd already placed a hefty order for a house white to keep stocked at the inn.

The red camera light blinked off, and she let herself slump a little to relax her spine. "What's next?"

"Across the square, let's hit the coffee shop and the bakery," Roger suggested. "That'll probably take us until the opening ceremony starts." He squinted at her. "You need a touch-up."

"Thanks, you're looking like a peach yourself," she said cheerfully. He adjusted his backwards ball cap and rolled his eyes at her as Leah came over.

The ring on her friend's finger glinted in the afternoon sunlight as Angelica obediently tilted her head for a quick powder. Leah adjusted her hair under the tweed cap she'd paired with a matching blazer and jeans, then patted her shoulder fondly and disappeared again after a quick, sizzling exchange of glances with Roger.

"You're cute," Angelica called after her, getting a middle finger raised from a distance in return. The sparkling diamond next to it severely lessened the impact.

Angelica smiled, spotting Noah in the crowd near the stage that had been set up against the gazebo. He was pouring wine, of course. This year's promotional giveaway was a commemorative River Hill sampling cup cast in ceramic with the town's logo on the side. Angelica planned to steal several extras for the inn; they'd be great for the bathrooms. She was already plotting how to make Noah, Max, and Sean give her theirs.

She finished up her soundbite on the other half of the town square, and then set up against the brick wall of the Amory family's bakery to do her very last on-camera interview.

For season one, anyway.

The negotiations had gone *very* well. Jai was practically getting ready to build a tower of money to roll around in like Scrooge McDuck, and he was actively hunting for new clients who might fit the celebrity lifestyle TV bill. "Renovations! Cooking shows! Wellness gurus!" he'd shouted gleefully into the phone last night. "Send them all!"

She'd promised to give his card to anybody she met who fit the bill.

"And … we're rolling," Roger said, bringing her back to the present.

He and Leah were a central part of the plan to create her own little mini-empire; thanks to Jai's negotiating, they'd both received full-time offers from the network to match her own.

She smiled into the camera again. "I moved to River Hill to restart my life." It was true, and a good start for what she wanted to say. "After years in Hollywood, I needed something I could be passionate about to give me focus. I think a lot of people have that moment in their lives when they realize they're ready to find a career or a lifestyle they truly love, and I've been fortunate enough to have the opportunity to seek it out." She paused. "I spent three years waiting for the perfect property."

This was the part where they'd edit in footage of her flicking through real-estate listings and visiting houses. Never mind that it all had been shot last week. The magic of TV made everything seem real. Thank goodness she'd finally figured out what truly *was* real.

"When I found River Hill, and the Oakwell estate, I knew I'd found the place I could call home for the next phase of my life." Out of the corner of her eye, she saw movement, and realized that Noah was making his way toward her, regardless of the cameras or the crew. With a lift of her lips she felt in her heart, she kept speaking. "What I didn't expect was to find the home of my heart."

And then he was there, his arms around her waist, and he was kissing her, the crew was whooping, and a crowd was gathering in the square behind them, cheering. Faintly, she heard Roger tell somebody to keep rolling, and she smiled against Noah's lips.

Take that, test audiences.

River Hill is an unlikely place to launch a whiskey empire, but Irishman Iain Brennan's just reckless enough to make it work. Especially when he finds out the dark-haired artist he spent one glorious night with lives across in town. And since he's never said no to mixing business with pleasure, hiring her to design his labels means spending even more time together.

Naomi Klein may have put down roots in River Hill, but she's not looking for happily-ever-after. Just the idea of forever gives her hives. Which makes a rootless Irish wanderer in town for three months the perfect fling. And shocking her society mother? Just a bonus.

But as cozy autumn nights turn into lazy winter mornings, Iain and Naomi realize they've done the unthinkable and fallen in love! Neither are ready to settle down, but settling for a life without the other is out of the question. Or is it?

Keep reading for a sneak peek at Naomi and Iain's road to an unlikely forever in THE DISTILLER'S DARLING.

CHAPTER ONE

"*W*ell, *that* just happened." Naomi Klein sipped her champagne as she watched her date practically vault across the dance floor in pursuit of another woman. She smiled fondly.

Noah Bradstone was one of her best friends, and she had reason to know he was damned good in bed, but he was going to have to be a hell of a lot more than a nice dick in a tailored suit if he wanted to land Angelica Travis. The former actress was building a hotel next door to Noah's vineyard, and he'd fallen head over heels for her the second she yelled at him. *A man with mommy issues*, Naomi reflected with a grin.

"I'm not sure I believe what I just heard," came a female voice from next to her.

Speak of the devil.

Naomi turned to find Noah's mother, Bernice Winchester Bradstone. Bernice was also Naomi's mother's best friend; sleeping with Noah had always felt the tiniest bit incestuous—not that he'd noticed or cared. The man's ability to ignore the things other people stressed about was something Naomi found equally exasperating and endearing. It was one reason she hadn't put an end to their extracurriculars years before.

She'd been perfectly happy with their now-and-then friends-with-benefits situation, but she'd long suspected Noah needed more. Just not from her. Much as he pretended to be a footloose and fancy-free commitment-phobe, Noah wanted long-term … whether he knew it or not. He was chasing picket fences, and Naomi sincerely hoped Angelica would be the one to give them to him.

She, however, wanted nothing to do with any of that. Just thinking about being with one person for the rest of her life—or even the rest of the year—gave her hives.

"Not what you expected?" she asked Bernice.

The older woman pursed her lips, colored to perfection with Chanel's quintessential red. "Not at all."

"Disappointed?"

"Not exactly. It's always a surprise when your children find happiness in a way you don't expect. When you're the one who raised them, you think you know them." Her expression turned thoughtful. "But you want them to be happy, however they get there." She smiled, and patted Naomi's shoulder fondly. "You'll know what I mean someday."

Not likely.

Naomi kept a smile pasted on her face and nodded

vaguely. She had no interest in children whatsoever, and it wasn't because she just hadn't met The One, as her mother frequently asserted.

"I see my parents," she told Bernice, effectively cutting that line of conversation off at the pass. "Talk to you soon." She exchanged the customary cheek kiss and made her way across the room to find her parents, her brother, and his wife standing in a cluster near the finger food.

The Doctors Klein made an imposing pair. Her father was the head of cardiology at San Francisco General, and her brother looked like a younger, slightly more muscular clone. Both had thick, dark hair that lay in gentle waves tamed by expensive cuts, and each had a beautiful woman on his arm.

"Hey, Nay," her brother said. "Single again?"

She resisted the urge to flip him the bird. The only deviation Jacob had ever made from The Klein Plan was to marry Tanya Deuterhorn instead of the Nice Jewish Girl their parents had picked out for him, and since Tanya had immediately converted and was currently making raising their three children look easy *and* keeping the books part-time for Jacob's celebrity-studded plastic surgery practice, he'd been swiftly forgiven.

Naomi, on the other hand, had been deviating from The Plan since she was five years old, when she'd demanded to go to art camp instead of ballet class.

"I was already single," she answered.

"Please, don't remind me." Her mother raised the

back of her wrist to her forehead in a sign of mock distress. "What happened over there?"

Judith Klein was the perfect doctor's wife and the ultimate socialite. She and Bernice ran their inner circle with gilded fists, and the Founders' Ball was their cornerstone event. Naomi was well aware that the prodigal daughter's date fleeing her side was not a good look for the family. While Naomi didn't particularly care about the impression she gave, Noah didn't deserve her mother's censure.

"I think Noah's in love," she said with a grin.

"He ought to be in love with *you*," her mother answered stiffly. Their two mothers had been planning their wedding since Naomi and Noah had gotten stuck in an elevator together at her bat mitzvah.

"Please," Jacob said with a mock shudder. "Noah's a great guy, but there's literally nobody I want less as a brother-in-law."

"That's just because you don't like wine," his wife said. "That Prodigy Pinot he made a few years ago was incredible." Tanya was a fan of Stonewell Vineyards, Noah's winery, and was a loyal customer, something that made Naomi love her almost as much as the fact that she never tried to set her up on blind dates.

"Give me hard liquor anytime," Jacob said, raising the small, tulip-shaped glass in his hand to catch the light. "Have you tried this one, Dad?"

Their father nodded. "It's straight from Ireland. Your mother heard about it from one of her cronies." He gave his wife a fond smile to take the sting out of his words. "The only thing I ask in return for my presence at these things is good whiskey."

Naomi resisted the urge to snort. As though he wouldn't have been here anyway. He was gunning hard for the Chief of Staff position at the hospital, and every single member of the Board of Directors attended the Founders' Ball. There was a very good reason her mother co-chaired the gala committee. The Klein Plan, in full effect.

"I wouldn't mind buying some of it," Jacob said idly, swirling his glass again and lifting it to his nose.

"I'll get you the information, but I don't think it's available here yet," his mother replied impatiently. "Can we get back to the real issue here?"

"What issue?"

"Your sister."

"I'm an issue? Gee, thanks, Mom," Naomi said.

"Darling girl, you've been an issue all your life and you're proud of it," her mother said, fondness mixing with exasperation in her voice. "Noah Bradstone aside, are you ever going to settle down?"

"I'm totally settled!" Naomi protested. "I have a mortgage!" She'd bought a cute craftsman bungalow in River Hill a few years ago, having decided she needed a home base instead of constantly traveling back and forth between studio and gallery residencies. She still spent a lot of time away from home, but at least she had one. Every time she pulled into the driveway, she felt like an honest-to-goodness grownup. And the studio space she'd converted the attic into was gorgeous. Her art had definitely improved since then, and the galleries she routinely worked with seemed to agree—she'd already had to fend off one owner tonight. He was set on buying a sculpture she'd intended to auction off, but his offer hadn't been good enough to keep her from moving on to the hors d'oeuvres table.

Her mother sniffed. "A tiny house in that ridiculous tourist town."

"River Hill isn't a tourist town. It's just not San Francisco."

"Mom can't imagine anybody not wanting to live here," Jacob said, gesturing wide to indicate all the glitz and glamour surrounding them. "If you leave the city, you might see the outdoors and breathe air that doesn't smell like cars and piss. Can't have that."

His wife elbowed him. "Hush."

"If you'd ever actually *visit* River Hill, you'd like it, Mom," Naomi said. "Jacob and Tanya have been."

"There's a really good restaurant there," Tanya said supportively. "Right in the town square."

Her mother shuddered theatrically. "Any town small enough to have a square is too small for me."

It would certainly be too small for the both of them, Naomi thought. Heck, the seven square miles that made up *San Francisco* had been too small, which was one of the many reasons she'd made her home a couple of hours away in the first place. It was the exact right distance to keep her family at bay.

"And if you're not going to marry Noah, how are

you going to meet somebody all the way out there?" Her mother was still talking, unfortunately.

"Can we not argue about me meeting somebody in the middle of the Founders' Ball, please?"

"Why not? I thought it was an annual tradition." Her brother grinned.

"Shut up, Jacob," Naomi and her mother snapped in unison.

"Ah, there's the other annual tradition," her father said, and Tanya giggled.

"I hear you like our whiskey," a new voice interjected. Deep and smooth, it sounded rather like Jacob always said whiskey tasted.

Naomi turned, and found her mouth suddenly dry. The most delicious man she'd ever seen was standing next to her, holding three glasses of whiskey in one huge hand. He was nearly the same height she was in her black, strappy, four-inch heels, which made him shorter than her father and brother. Solidly built, he filled out his tux to perfection. Some attempt had been made to tame the brown beard that rose above the snowy white points of his shirt, but nothing could disguise the laugh lines carved deep around his eyes. A few freckles were visible beneath his light tan, and his hair had been artfully mussed. The muscles in his broad shoulders shifted, and she glanced down at the drinks he was offering them. Somehow, his palm managed to cradle the bases of all three glasses while his fingers balanced between their edges, holding them safely. She stared blankly at his hand, feeling a tiny zinging sensation down her spine that led straight to curiosity: what would those hands feel like on *her*?

Naomi managed to drag her eyes back up to his face, which didn't help much, because his warm blue eyes were on her, too. She wondered if he was thinking the same wickedly delicious thoughts.

"I don't like whiskey," she blurted, and his eyes crinkled in an easy smile.

Passing two glasses to her father and brother, the man held onto the third. "Is that so?"

She shrugged, attempting to recapture her usual cool. "Sorry, never have."

"It would be an acquired taste," he said, raising the glass to his nose with an easy swirl before inhaling. "But I came out of the womb reaching for a dram." His Irish accent was obvious now, and she found herself wanting to hear him talk more.

Jacob snorted. "An acquired taste. Sounds like you, sis."

"Are you done?" she snapped, feeling heat rising in her cheeks—and elsewhere.

Her silk dress—which put the 'little' in little black dress—didn't leave much to the imagination, and if she didn't quickly bring her body's reactions under control, the sexy stranger trying to ply her with booze was going to know *exactly* how she responded to him. She could feel her nipples turning into hard little points beneath the thin fabric.

Although maybe that wasn't such a bad thing, she thought, letting her gaze roam over him again as he exchanged pleasantries with her family. It had been a while since she'd come across someone who made her heart beat like a herd of wild horses running at full gallop, and this man—with his rugged good looks and Irish accent that was out of place in this posh San Francisco ballroom—certainly qualified in that regard.

Naomi didn't spend a lot of time in society, but when she did, she felt nearly as much of a stranger as he seemed to be. She'd escaped her parents' inner circle a long time ago, and these days she was accustomed to a much more private way of life. One that didn't mean she had to pretend to be meek and demure and wait for men to get around to thinking about *her* wants and desires. She had an active sex drive, and she used it well and often, something her mother would probably be horrified to know. As far as Naomi was concerned, as long as everybody involved was a consenting adult and nobody was married, she was more than happy with the way things were.

She might be even happier if she could convince the sexy Irishman to join her for a nightcap. Provided, of course, it wasn't whiskey.

CHAPTER TWO

*J*ain surveyed the sexy American with renewed interest. He'd been eyeing her all evening. Hearing her give as good as she got had him itching to know more about her. The woman had fire. And he liked it.

"At the risk of sounding like a cliche," Iain whispered, shifting closer to her side while her brother laughed about a joke he'd just told at her expense, "can I get you a drink—one that's not my family's whiskey?"

She glanced at her parents, who were in deep conversation with the other couple, and shrugged. "Sure, that'd be great." Without saying goodbye, she turned and walked away, clearly expecting Iain to follow.

Which he was more than happy to do. She was stunning from the front, but the back of her dress—a network of criss-crossed silver beaded strands that shimmered with each step she took—was a work of art that rippled over her flesh, hugging her in all the right places.

Iain lengthened his stride to catch up and held out his hand. "I'm Iain, by the way. I'm afraid I didn't catch your name back there."

Moving into a corner where they were partially hidden from the crowd by a potted palm, she stuck out her hand in return. "Naomi. And it's nice to meet you."

Iain took Naomi's hand in his, and was unnerved to feel an instant, white-hot bolt of ... something ... travel straight to his gut. He didn't believe in love at first sight, but there was definitely *something* between them. Some unexplainable chemistry he'd never felt with anyone before—and he was desperate to explore it further.

Preferably somewhere her family *wasn't* nearby, and a bed *was*.

"About that drink I promised—"

"—What do you say we get out of here, and go somewhere less stuffy?" she interrupted before he could suggest the very same thing.

They smiled at one another, and then Naomi looked away briefly before setting her fingers to her mouth. Dropping her hand, she said, "I'm sorry. That probably sounded awfully forward." She didn't sound particularly sorry, though, Iain noted.

"Not at all." He grinned. "In fact, I was just about to ask if you wanted to get out of here. I know this little bar down the street that makes the best cocktails—"

"Gibson's?" she asked, her eyes catching the light and twinkling like the crystal in the chandeliers above.

"Yeah, you know it?"

"Oh, Iain," she laughed, setting her hand to his arm. "Everyone knows Gibson's. It's the hottest place in town right now."

"Oh." He should have known she would already know all the best places in San Francisco. That he'd honestly thought he'd stumbled on an undiscovered gem after spending thirty minutes with the barman earlier that afternoon made him feel a bit foolish. He should have known better. After all, he'd practically *been* that barman once.

She stepped out of their alcove and tossed him a smile over her shoulder. "Come on, let's grab my wrap and we can head out. If you like Gibson's, I'll show you somewhere even better."

Thirty minutes later, they were tucked into a dark booth in the back of a bar Iain wasn't sure should still be standing. The floor was slanted, the walls were bowed, and the patchy ceiling wasn't much taller than the woman sitting next to him. He'd been in some questionable establishments over the years—including a pub built into a cave where monks used to hide out from raiding hordes—but this one took the prize for 'most likely to crumble in on itself.'

Looking around, he blew out a whistle. "This is …"

"A death trap?" She laughed again, a warm sound he was growing to enjoy.

Once they'd left the ball, Naomi's whole demeanor had changed. Her shoulders had instantly relaxed, and her eyes looked less wary, like she wasn't constantly on guard. She hadn't said anything, but he got the sense she didn't enjoy those fancy events nearly as much as her family wished she might. Honestly, he could relate.

"That's exactly what I was going to say."

"Yeah, I'm pretty sure if there's a bad earthquake, we're dead." She looked around the joint, her face happy and her eyes bright. "Although, come to think of it, this building's been here since before 1906, so we're probably safe."

"1906? Oh, the earthquake?" Upon touching down in San Francisco last week, Iain had quickly learned there were three topics of conversation you could safely embark on if you found yourself in conversation

with a stranger here: the weather (it was great), tech-
nology (it was either life-changing or the root of all
evil, depending on your audience), and when "the big
one" might hit. Apparently, there'd been something
everyone called "a four-point-two" the day before he'd
landed, causing some damage in Berkeley, and it had
people on edge.

"One and the same," she said, tossing back the last
of her gin and tonic. Iain didn't like to brag, but he
thought the gin his family made was slightly more
flavorful. Then again, he supposed he wasn't at all
impartial.

"I can't imagine living like that, always on the verge
of disaster without any warning."

"Oh, it's not too bad. The worst we've had since
1989 is a little bit of the bed rocking in the middle of
the night." There was a beat of silence, then Naomi's
eyes went wide with recognition at what she'd just said.
She laughed again. "Oh, no, you probably think ..."

Iain eyed her over the rim of his glass. "That you
have a fantastic sense of humor and are utterly delightful. Not to mention incredibly beautiful."

She eyed him back, her expression quickly shifting
from jovial to thoughtful. "I'm just going to put this out
there—and you can tell me I'm insane for even
suggesting it—but do you want to go back to my
hotel?"

Iain tried to play it cool, but he was definitely
surprised. He'd been hoping that's how the night would
end, but he'd assumed he'd be the one to make a move

… a few hours from now. From the time they'd walked through the door of the pub, he'd known he was going to fuck Naomi, he just hadn't known *when*. He was confident in who he was. He was never going to be the best-looking lad in the room, but he had something no other man here did: an Irish accent. Personally, he didn't see what the big deal was, but across several continents, it was a sure-fire panty-dropper.

He set his glass to the side and captured her gaze. "Just so I'm clear here, you're asking me back to your room so we can make the bed do a little rocking in the middle of the night?" His lips hitched to the side in a smirk, while hers did the same. He appreciated that she appreciated his bad joke.

"Yes, exactly. I'd also like to make the walls rattle a bit, if you're up for it."

"You really are the most delightful woman I've ever met," he said, sliding out of the booth and tossing a handful of bills on the sticky table before reaching out and taking her hand. "I promise to do my best to bring security down on our heads."

As they stumbled out onto the sidewalk, a dense fog snaked its way around them, wrapping their bodies in a misty cold. Naomi shivered, and pulled her flimsy black wrap tighter around her bare arms. Iain stepped behind her and circled her middle with his arms. With her hair up in an intricate knot, he had perfect access to her neck.

"I've been wanting to taste you here all night," he said, dropping a soft, open-mouthed kiss to the skin just below her ear. "And here," he added, dotting kisses up the length of her long, delicate neck.

She shivered once more, and this time not from the cold. "Do that again."

His tongue flicked out and licked a path from her spine to her nape. "If you taste this sweet here," he said, trailing his lips along her shoulder, "I can't wait to taste you here." His hand skated its way down, down, down.

"Oh God, that's hot." She melted into his embrace. "Where's that damn Uber?"

"Where's your hotel?"

She jutted out her chin. "Down the hill, in SoMA."

Damn. They definitely needed a cab. There was no way Naomi was walking that far in those spikes she called shoes. Reluctantly dragging his lips from her heated skin, Iain scanned their surroundings. He couldn't be sure, but he *thought* they might not be too far from where he was staying.

"Is this Nob Hill?"

She chuckled. "Sure. Or the Tender-Nob. Or the Nobber-Loin. Take your pick."

"How far is Union Square?"

"A couple of blocks. Why?"

He pulled her in tight against him. Tight enough, he knew, that she'd be able to feel his erection straining against his trousers. He wanted this woman, and she wanted him. And neither of them wanted to wait. "I'm staying at the Westin. We could—"

Before he had time to explain his line of thinking, Naomi had stepped out of his hold, grabbed his hand,

and was marching them quickly down the street. He'd never seen a woman move so quickly and so effortlessly in shoes like that, but he wasn't about to complain. Clearly, she wanted this as much as he did.

"I—"

"Shh, no talking." She shot him an apologetic smile. "Sorry, that was rude. I'm just super keyed up right now and I don't want to lose that feeling. We'll be in your hotel room in approximately ten minutes, and hopefully you'll be inside of me a few minutes after that. I don't want to make it awkward with small talk."

Christ. What was that he'd thought earlier about love at first sight? Because the more he got to know Naomi, the more he liked about her. Actually, honestly liked. When you factored in her no-bullshit stance toward sex, he thought he might even be half in love with her. All in the course of one evening. Provided that sort of thing actually happened in real life. But since it didn't, he pulled her hand to his lips and kissed her palm, his tongue flicking out at the last second to give her a brief preview of what she could expect in approximately thirteen minutes.

Because while he couldn't wait to sink his cock inside of her, he didn't want to rush things either. He'd told her he wanted to taste her, and he hadn't been lying. Iain had a very refined palate, and he planned to spend several long moments identifying all the unique flavors that comprised Miss Naomi.

When she moaned and squeezed his hand in a vice

grip before increasing their pace, Iain chuckled to himself. *Yeah, we're on the exact same page.*

Six minutes later (but who was counting?) they sailed through the doors of the hotel and into the grand lobby. Without breaking stride, Naomi made her way straight to the elevator bay, and pressed the button.

"You come here often?" Iain felt an unexpected bolt of jealousy. He knew this was a one-night stand and that they were both sexual beings, but he didn't like the reminder of just *how* sexual Naomi might actually be. That probably made him a chauvinist pig, but he didn't think she'd want to be confronted with the evidence of his past partners either.

Her eyes found his, and immediately the heat in them cooled. "Yes, many times. Is that a problem?"

He didn't like the implication of that frosty statement, but he liked the idea of them parting ways even less. He didn't want to say goodbye without learning just how hot their fire burned. If it was even half as potent as he thought it might be, their night together would be worth it. And besides, it wasn't like he was going to marry this girl; what, and who, they'd done before they'd met had no bearing on the things they were about to do to one another in the here and now. All he needed to do now was wrap it up and enjoy the ride.

"No problem at all," he said as the door chimed and then slid open. Placing his hand on the small of her back, over where her dress dipped deliciously low in the back, he guided her inside the compartment.

When the doors shut, he pressed the button for his floor and she turned to him. "I don't come here to—"

He stepped into her space, backing her up against the wall. "It doesn't matter," he growled, nipping at her lush bottom lip and tugging it between his teeth. "I want you, and I intend to have you. I don't care about anything else."

Naomi's head fell back with a moan, and she speared her fingers through his hair, holding him close while he feasted on her skin. With his attention focused on her dainty collar bone, Iain slid the strap of her dress down her shoulder where it pooled at her elbow. The obsidian fabric slipped down her skin with a slight whoosh, exposing her nipple to his hungry mouth. When he sucked it between his lips, she mewled, the sound going straight to his dick.

"Has anyone ever told you that you have an exceptionally talented mouth?" she asked, her words coming out in between pants and moans.

He flicked the pert, dusky pink nub with his tongue and winked. "You ain't seen nothing yet."

THE BAKER'S BEAUTY
(River Hill #3)

After tragedy struck, Sean Amory left L.A. to come home to River Hill to work in his family's bakery. The familiar surroundings soothe his raw nerves while the gorgeous brunette who jogs past every morning has another effect entirely. And when she helps him out of a bind, he learns that Jess is even sweeter than the apple fritters he's become famous for.

Former beauty queen Jessica Casillas-Moore hasn't eaten carbs since she was fourteen, but that doesn't stop her from jogging past The Breadery every morning. And when she meets the handsome baker who works there, Sean is every bit as mouthwatering as the pastries he serves—and so much better for her waistline.

But between her family's disapproval and his haunting past, the odds seem stacked against them. Can they learn to trust in each other and their growing love, or is their relationship a recipe for disaster?

THE BARISTA'S BELOVED
(River Hill #4)

It's been months since whiskey maker Maeve Brennan has been on a date, and she's coming dangerously close to giving up on men altogether—until she crosses paths with River Hill's sexy new barista. But Ben's made it clear he only wants to be friends, so Maeve will definitely stop fantasizing about his forearms that put Captain America to shame. Probably. Maybe.

Former lawyer Ben Worthington never thought he'd be living above his best friend's garage and slinging coffee, but there's a lot about his life that doesn't make sense. Like his attraction to the town's beloved distiller. But since Maeve's made it clear she doesn't have time for romance, Ben will stop dreaming about her naked. Soon. Eventually.

But when the youth center where Maeve volunteers comes under fire from a big-city developer, Ben realizes he's exactly the type of hero she needs. He just hopes she can live with his take-no-prisoners approach to winning, because he's pretty sure he can't live without her.

ACKNOWLEDGMENTS

From Rebecca

As always, thanks to my husband who offers endless encouragement and never rolls his eyes when I say, "I have an idea for another book."

Thank you to our beta readers who loved Angelica and Noah as much as we did, and who've only mildly harassed us about when they can get their hands on the next installments.

A huge shout out to the many book bloggers who've supported me along the way and have been enthusiastic about the River Hill Series since I teased you with the words "sexy winemaker" almost a year ago. Your support does not go unnoticed.

And finally, a huge thank you to Jamaila, who just might be my soul sister. When I first said I was thinking about writing this series, she immediately wanted to know if Angelica could pretty please renovate a historic home. Since that was *exactly* what I'd planned, it was like this partnership was meant to be. Needless to say, it's been the most seamless writing experience of my career. Now let's get back to work!

From Jamaila

Special thanks and a hundred kisses to my husband, who has put up with writers' retreats, frenetic emails, and a LOT of giggling. He's also stocked our wine rack and stuck with me through multiple home renovations, much of which he did himself. He's a keeper!

More thanks to our beta readers, who made grabby hands at us until we finished this book already, darn it!

And the bloggers and PR friends who have helped us throughout, and continue to wax enthusiastic about River Hill and everyone in it.

And finally, of course, a hundred thanks to Rebecca, who came up with this idea and thought co-writing might be a fun thing to do. Turns out: it is. I had the most fun writing this book that I've ever had writing. Can't wait for more.

The Rocky Cove Series
Not Quite Perfect
A Perfect Mistake
Second Time Around

The Dublin Rugby Romance Series
Coming Home
First Comes Love
Just For Now
Take A Chance On Me
Forever At Last

The Billionaire Series
The Contract
The Boss

The McClintock Security Series

Bound To Me
Return To Me

Steamy Standalones
Hollywood Dreams
Secrets and Lies

THE WIZARDS OF LONDON SERIES
Thieves' Honor
Witch's Stone
Captain's Lady

THE GALIPP FILES
The Star of Anatolia
The Mathematical Gambit
The Portrait Problem

ABOUT THE AUTHORS

Rebecca Norinne and Jamaila Brinkley have been friends for almost fifteen years. Separately, they write contemporary romance and historical fantasy romance; together, they created the enchanting world of River Hill. In this charming Northern California town, Norinne and Brinkley combined the interests that made them friends in the first place—great food, delicious wine, and a pinch of home renovation—and added in the spicy romance they love.

Rebecca lives in Massachusetts with her husband, and Jamaila lives in Maryland with her husband and twin children. They email each other a lot.